Lily Robbins, M.D.
(Medical Dabbler)

Other Books in the Young Women of Faith Library

The Lily Series
Here's Lily!
Lily Robbins, M.D. (Medical Dabbler)
Lily and the Creep
Lily's Ultimate Party
Ask Lily
Lily the Rebel
Lights, Action, Lily!
Lily Rules!
Lily Speaks!

Nonfiction
The Beauty Book
The Body Book
The Buddy Book
The Best Bash Book
The Blurry Rules Book
The It's MY Life Book
The Creativity Book
The Uniquely Me Book
The Year 'Round Holiday Book
The Values & Virtues Book
Dear Diary
Girlz Want to Know
NIV Young Women of Faith Bible
YWOF Journal: Hey! This Is Me
Take It from Me

Young Women of Faith

Lily Robbins, M.D.
(Medical Dabbler)

Nancy Rue

Zonder**kidz**

We want to hear from you. Please send your comments about this book to us in care of the address below. Thank you.

Zonder**kidz**™

Grand Rapids, MI 49530
www.zonderkidz.com

Zonder**kidz**™
The children's group of Zondervan

Lily Robbins, M.D.
Copyright © 2000 by Women of Faith

Requests for information should be addressed to:
Zonderkidz, *Grand Rapids, Michigan 49530*
www.zonderkidz.com

ISBN: 0-310-23249-X

Published in association with the literary agency of Alive Communications, Inc., 7680 Goddard Street, Suite 200, Colorado Springs, CO 80920.

Interior design by Amy E. Langeler

Printed in the United States of America

03 04 05 06 /❖ DC/ 22 21 20 19 18 17 16 15 14 13 12 11

Chapter
1

"Psst! Snobbins!"

Lily Robbins didn't have to look up from the pizza boxes she was carrying to know that voice. It was Shad Shifferdecker—the most obnoxious kid in the entire sixth grade. She tossed her mane of red hair and, as usual, ignored him.

And, as usual, he persisted. That was one of the things that made him so obnoxious.

"Snobbins!" he hissed again. "Are you gonna eat all that pizza yourself? Dude!"

Lily just kept moving toward the door out of Little Caesar's. *Just a couple more steps and I'll be away from the absurd little creep,* she told herself. *And the sooner the better.*

She leaned against the glass door and pushed herself out into the January-freezing air.

"See ya tomorrow," Shad said behind her. "If you can get through the classroom door—"

The door slapped shut, and Lily hurried toward the maroon van where her mom was waiting with the motor running and the heater blasting. But even though Lily couldn't hear him anymore, she knew Shad wasn't finished with her. He never was.

Don't look back, she warned herself. *Or you'll see something gross.*

Still, just as she reached the van she caught a glimpse of her mom's face. It was twisted up into a question mark as she stared inside Little Caesar's. Lily couldn't help it. She took a glance over her shoulder—and immediately wished she hadn't.

There was Shad at the door, his whole jacket crammed inside his T-shirt and his cheeks puffed out to three times their normal size so that he looked like a demented version of the Pillsbury doughboy.

You are so *not funny!* Lily wanted to shout at him.

Instead she flipped her head around and stomped toward the van. Or, at least she *tried* to. On her second step, her heel slid on the ice, and she careened crazily forward, juggling pizza boxes and heading for a collision with the frozen ground.

The pizzas hit first with Lily right on top of them. She could feel the warmth of the grease through the box against her cheek. The smell of pepperoni went right up her nose.

Above her she could hear the van window on the passenger side going down.

"You all right, Lil?" Mom said.

"Yeah," Lily answered through her teeth.

"Is the pizza all right?"

Lily moaned and peeled herself off the pile of slightly flattened boxes. "I bet all the topping is stuck to the cardboard now," she said.

"Don't worry about it," Mom said. "Just get in the van before you freeze your buns off—and our dinner gets cold."

Lily did, although she wasn't as worried about her buns *or* the pizza as she was about the story Shad Shifferdecker was going to spread to their whole class tomorrow. But she didn't even risk a glance inside Little Caesar's as she climbed into the van and examined the top pizza.

"I think it's okay," she said while Mom was backing out of the parking place and mercifully leaving Shad behind. "Just some pepperoni stuck to the lid, but I can peel that off."

"And I would if I were you," Mom said dryly, "before your brothers get a look at it and want to know what happened."

"Mom, please don't—"

"How much is it worth to you for me to keep my mouth shut?"

Mom's mouth was twitching the way it always did when she was teasing. She never smiled that much, although the twinkle in her big brown doe-eyes usually gave her away.

"You're not gonna tell," Lily said.

"Who was that delightful child in the pizza place?" Mom said, lips still twitching. "Friend of yours?"

"No, he is NOT! Gross!"

"Come on, now, Lil, don't hold back. Tell me how you really feel."

"I can't stand Shad Shifferdecker," Lily said, inspecting pizza #2. "He can*not* leave me alone—he's in my face all the time, telling me my hair looks like it's on fire or my mouth looks like Mick Jagger's or my skin's so white it blinds him out in the sun."

"Charming," Mom said. "How's the one with the works? Art will go ballistic if his sausage is mixed up with his Canadian bacon."

Lily pried open the lid to the pizza on the bottom and wrinkled her nose. "How do you know whether it's messed up or not?" she said. "It always looks like somebody already ate it to me, with all that stuff on there—"

"Lily, hold on!"

Mom's arm came out and flattened against Lily's chest. The van swerved sharply, and suddenly felt as if it were out of control. Lily looked up just in time to see a pair of taillights in front of them disappear as the car spun around. Headlights glared in their faces.

"Mom!" Lily screamed.

She squeezed her eyes shut and, for some reason she could never figure out, clutched the pizza boxes against her. She felt the van lurch to a stop, and she waited for the crash that was surely going to kill them both. But all she heard was her mother's gasp.

"Oh, dear Lord!"

Lily opened her eyes again. The other car had spun once more and was sailing across the road, straight toward a pickup truck coming from the other direction. As Lily and her mother watched, the two vehicles slammed together and crumpled like—like two pizza boxes. Metal smashed. Glass broke. And then it was as quiet as snow itself.

"Dear Lord," Mom said again. Only this time her voice was quiet and grim as she reached for the car phone and punched in three numbers.

"Do you think anybody got hurt?" Lily said.

She knew the answer was obvious, but it was the only thing that came into her head.

"There's been an accident on Route 130," Mom was saying into the phone.

How could somebody not *get hurt in that?* Lily thought. She shuddered and tried not to think of what the people inside must look like.

Mom hung up the phone and grabbed her gloves. "I'm going to go see if I can do anything before the paramedics get here."

"You're going *over* there?" Lily said.

"I'd want somebody to come help us if we'd been the ones that got hit." Mom pulled her knit cap down over her ponytail. "And we almost were."

A chill went through Lily, and it wasn't from the blast of frosty air that came in as her mother opened the van door. *It* could *have been us—all crumpled up and maybe bleeding—*

It wasn't a thought she wanted to be left alone with. She got out of the van and followed her mother, picking her way across the ice.

"Lil, why don't you stay here until I know what's happened," Mom said.

"I want to come," Lily said. Her own voice sounded thin and scared.

"Then get some blankets out of the back—and the first-aid kit."

Lily didn't even know there *was* a first-aid kit in the van. It didn't strike her as a Mom kind of thing. Whenever Lily or her younger brother, Joe, or her older brother, Art, got hurt, Mom would say, "Are you hemorrhaging? Have a bone sticking out?" When the answer was no, she'd tell them to go get a Band-Aid and not whine about it.

But there *was* a first-aid kit in the back of the van, along with two blankets and even a pillow. Lily grabbed all of it and made her way over to the side of the road.

Mom was there with some other people who had stopped, and they were all crouched around somebody on the ground. As soon as Lily got close, Mom put her hand up and said, "That's far enough, Lil. Just leave the stuff here."

There was no merry twitching around her mother's mouth now. Her tan face was white, and her voice was strained. Lily backed away, heart pounding.

"Could we have one of those blankets over here?" someone said.

Lily looked up. There was a teenage boy, around Art's age, crouched down beside a small person. The child was sitting up—it was safe to go over there. Lily grabbed one of the blankets she'd just set down and slipped and slid across the ice to get to them.

"I don't think he's hurt," the teenager said to Lily, "but he's shaking like he's freezing."

Lily squatted beside him. A boy of about five blinked up at Lily out of a face the color of cream of wheat. His lips were blue, and the teenager was right: He was trembling like a leaf about to fall off a tree.

"You want a blanket?" Lily said to him.

9

He didn't answer, but Lily wrapped it around him anyway and then rubbed her hands up and down his arms, the way her dad did to her when she was whining about being in danger of frostbite if she had to walk to school.

"I don't think he's hurt," the teenager said again. "He's probably not, huh?"

Lily looked up at him in surprise. He was shaking as badly as the little boy was, and even in the dark Lily could see tears shimmering in his eyes.

"He doesn't look like he is," Lily said.

"Nah—I bet he's not."

The teen crossed his arms over his chest and stuck his hands into his armpits. His bottom lip was vibrating.

"Did you ask him?" Lily said.

"He won't say nothin'! He just sits there—but he's probably not hurt."

The teenager just kept shaking his head. Lily got a strange feeling, like the kid didn't really know what he was saying. Mouth suddenly dry, Lily turned to the little boy.

"What's your name?" she said.

The little blue lips came open. "Thomas," he said in a voice she could hardly hear.

"I'm Lily," she said.

"Lily," he said.

The teenager let out a shrill laugh. "You see! He's not hurt, huh?"

"Do you have any *owies*, Thomas?" Lily said.

"What's an 'owie'?" the teenage boy said.

But before Lily had a chance to say, "You know, boo-boo, a cut or a scrape or something—" the air was filled with the screaming of sirens. The teenager's face drained, and his eyes went wild.

"I just lost control!" he said. "It was the ice—I couldn't help it!"

His voice was so frightened, even little Thomas started to cry. Lily put her hands on his arms to rub them again, but he stuck his own arms out and hurled himself against her. There was nothing to do but fold him up in a hug.

"It's okay, Thomas," Lily said to him. "You're okay."

The teenage boy was *not* okay. The minute a police officer got out of his car and started toward him, the kid broke into tears. It made Lily feel like she wanted to be somewhere else. Fortunately, the policeman took him aside.

But then little Thomas started to whimper.

"You're okay," Lily said. "You aren't hurt. It's okay—"

"I am too hurt," Thomas said.

Lily pulled him away from her a little and looked at him. "Where?" she said.

"My tummy," he said. "It hurts a lot."

"Oh," Lily said.

She looked around for someone to call to, but the flock of uniformed adults who had just arrived all seemed to be either running around or hovering around the person on the ground. Lily looked back at Thomas. He was leaning over at the middle now, and his eyes were looking funny, like he couldn't quite focus them.

"Um ... why don't you lie down and I'll get somebody to help us," Lily said.

"Don't leave!" Thomas said, and he clutched at her sleeve with his fingers. Lily noticed for the first time that he didn't have gloves on, and his little fingers were red and stiff.

"Okay, but lie down. And put these on."

She peeled off her knit mittens and slid them over his tiny hands. Then she got him to curl up in the blanket with his head in her lap.

"You smell like pizza," he murmured.

It was the kind of voice a person used when he was about to fall asleep, and it scared Lily. She twisted around and caught sight of a paramedic walking away from the person on the ground, right toward them.

"This one's okay?" the paramedic called to her.

"I don't think so," Lily called back. "He says his stomach hurts. And his eyes look funny and his lips are blue and he's falling asleep."

The paramedic's steps got faster, and he already had his little flashlight out when he got to them.

"Hey, fella," he said to Thomas as he shined the light in his eyes.

"His name's Thomas," Lily said.

"Stretcher over here!" the paramedic called out. "We're gonna have to take you to the hospital, Thomas," he said.

"Mommy!" Thomas said.

"Mommy's going, too, only she's getting a different ride. You'll see her when you get there."

"You come with me."

Thomas was looking right at Lily, his eyes trying hard to stay focused.

"Is this your sister?" the paramedic said.

"I didn't even know him before tonight," Lily said.

The paramedic grinned. "He sure likes you." He went on doing things to Thomas as he talked. "Thanks for staying here with him. The other driver told us he thought he was all right." He grunted softly. "'Course, he has a reason to want him to be all right."

Thomas whimpered, and Lily leaned down over him. "You *will* be all right, Thomas," she said.

"Sure he will. All right, fella—we're gonna put you on this stretcher and give you a wild ride. How would you like that?"

Thomas's face puckered weakly. "I want *her* to take me."

"Tell you what," said the paramedic as two other people in navy blue down jackets lifted Thomas like he was a feather and put him on a stretcher. "She can walk with us to the ambulance. How would that be?"

Thomas nodded, and Lily scrambled to her feet and got as close to the stretcher as she could without getting in the way of the IV bottle that was already suspended above him. She knew what that was—she'd had one herself last fall. It was much better being on this side of the stretcher. She could put her hand out to Thomas and hold his as she hurried along to the ambulance, and she could talk to him and reassure him that everything really was going to be okay.

He still wailed for her when they slid him inside the ambulance—and she would have jumped right in there with him if any of them had given her half a chance. But they closed the doors behind him, and the first paramedic put his hand on Lily's shoulder just before he headed for the driver's seat.

"Thanks for your help," he said.

Then he jumped into the front of the ambulance, the siren wound up, and they pulled out of the icy slush and back onto Route 130.

As Lily watched them go, she could almost hear the paramedic adding, "And, Lily, you're welcome on our team anytime."

Chapter 2

As the ambulance disappeared amid the traffic, Lily felt a pang inside.

I wish I could have gone with Thomas, she thought. *I want to know what happens to him. After all, I was the one who discovered he was actually hurt. They might even let me help—since I'm the one he wants anyway—*

"You okay, Lil?"

Mom was suddenly beside her. Her face was still white, but her voice sounded normal again. "I'm sorry you had to see all that."

"No—I'm fine!" Lily said. "Can we go to the hospital?"

Mom's lips twitched. "Why? Don't you think the doctors can handle it without you?"

"Mo-om!" Lily said.

Mom put her arm around Lily's shoulders and gave them a squeeze. "I'm just teasing you. I was watching you, and you actually handled yourself very well. You know how to keep your head in an emergency. I was impressed."

Lily managed to mumble a "thanks." Her mind was already spinning a vision.

I could be a rescuer and healer, she thought. *I could learn first aid and just, like, be there whenever there was an accident and take care of people until the paramedics got there.* The thoughts spun on—*I could keep them from losing hope. I could find the injuries nobody else could detect*—

"I bet those pizzas are ice-cold by now," she heard her mother say as she started the van. "I better call your dad and let him know what's going on—if he's even missed us!"

Lily's dad tended to lose track of things when he was absorbed in a book, which he usually was, being a college English literature professor and all that.

But Lily's brothers had missed them. They were waiting at the garage door that led into the laundry room/mud room practically with their plates in hand.

"We got the oven heated up," Art said, grabbing for the pizza boxes Lily was carrying. "We can warm these babies right up."

"How can you think about food after what we've just been through?" Lily said.

"You got in a traffic jam because of an accident," Art said.

"Big deal," Joe said. "You didn't eat it all while you were sitting there, did you?"

Lily rolled her eyes and flounced on into the kitchen. Mom's lips were twitching, but she did say, "We weren't just hanging around in the traffic, guys. We were the first people on the scene. We had to help."

"We?" Art said as he opened the box to the works and scrutinized the damages to his pizza. "What did you do, Lily?"

He didn't add, "Get in the way?" Mom and Dad didn't let the kids say mean stuff to each other anymore.

"She was cool," Mom said. "She kept a little kid with internal injuries from freaking out until the paramedics got there."

Wow, Lily thought. *So, like, I helped save Thomas's life?*

As pizzas were stuffed into the oven for warm-up and Dad and Art and Joe waited impatiently at the table, Mom filled them in on the whole event. Lily's mind, of course, spiraled off.

Maybe I could know more than just first aid, she thought. *What about CRP? Or is it CPR? I'd have to find out . . .*

But why stop there? Why not just become, like—a doctor? *I could wear a white coat, and I could say things like "STAT!"*

It was all there in her mind—herself clad in white, breezing into a hospital room and saying crisply, "Let's have a look at that chart," while nurses and paramedics ran around filling her orders and watching in admiration.

"Lil, aren't you going to eat?" Mom said.

Lily looked up to find a piece of worn-out-looking pizza on a plate in front of her.

"I'll take it if she doesn't want it," Joe said. At nine, he was always either eating or bouncing a basketball.

"Nope, it's mine," said Art. He, too, was what Mom called a "bottomless pit." If he wasn't doing something with his saxophone, he was standing at the refrigerator yelling, "There's nothing to eat!"

Lily pushed her plate toward him. "You can have it," she said. "I'm gonna go call Reni, okay?"

"What are ya gonna call her?" Joe said. That was his joke of the week.

Lily ignored it and went for the portable phone in the family room which she took to her own room and locked the door—thereby following two of her sacred rules. One, you call your best friend and tell her important things as soon as you can after they happen. And, two, you do it in total privacy, because brothers don't always think what you consider important is really important—and they tease you until you scream.

Lily leaned back against China, her giant stuffed panda, and dialed the phone.

"Hello?" Reni said.

"You aren't going to believe what happened to me tonight!" Lily said.

That was the way it was with best friends. You didn't have to bother with a bunch of "Hi, how are ya" stuff, especially when you had something *way* exciting to share.

Lily did share it, with all the suspense buildup and precise detail she could muster. Reni listened with rapt attention—the way a best friend was supposed to. She punctuated the tale with her usual, "No, you did not!" and "No, he did not!" which only meant, "This is too exciting to believe!" It spurred Lily on to make the story even more delicious.

"Did you call Suzy or Zooey or Kresha?" Reni said when Lily was finally finished.

"'Course not," Lily said. "I called you first, naturally. I'll probably tell them tomorrow."

"Do we have a meeting?"

"Uh-huh. Did I tell you that the paramedic thanked me for my help?"

"Yes, you did. Two times, I think."

"No, he only said it once."

"I was talking about you. *You* told me twice. So what do you think we should do at the meeting? Mama made some brownies tonight, so I could bring those."

Lily plucked at China's fur. She really wanted to talk about the accident some more. She hadn't gotten to the part where she'd decided to become a doctor yet. That was the best part.

"So do you want me to bring the brownies?" Reni said.

"Bring them where?"

"To the Girlz Only meeting, silly!"

"Oh," Lily said. But the mention of the Girlz Only Group suddenly gave her an idea. "Bring them!" she said. "Yeah—and I know just what we should talk about at the meeting."

"What?" Reni's voice stopped sounding bored. "Tell me!"

"Nope," Lily said. "It's a surprise."

"Oh." There was a long pause on the other end of the phone. Then Lily heard Reni sniff. "I *am* the vice president, you know."

"I know," Lily said. "But I want it to be a surprise. I mean, I'm the president—"

"Okay, fine, never mind," Reni said.

Pretty soon they hung up, and for a minute Lily felt a little funny, kind of the way you do when you just stepped on somebody's toe and you didn't mean to.

But the vision that was already forming in Lily's head reassured her. She could just see herself explaining their new focus to the Girlz—Suzy and Zooey and Kresha and Reni. She could picture Zooey's round face going all red with excitement and Kresha babbling happily in Croatian and Suzy actually smiling instead of giving that nervous little giggle she used when she wasn't quite sure of herself.

But best of all, she could imagine Reni completely forgetting that she was irritated with Lily as her dimples deepened and she pulled her chin in and said, "Girl, you are *good!*"

Lily was so wired up when she went to bed she couldn't fall asleep, which was okay, because that gave her time to pray. Ever since last fall when she had had her own accident, she tried to take everything to God.

"Lord?" she whispered as she snuggled down into bed with China. "Would you please help me become a great healer?" Later she fell asleep and dreamed about Joe and Art in white coats grabbing pizzas from her and yelling, "Get these in the oven—STAT!"

Chapter 3

"Wow, Mom," Lily said at the breakfast table the next morning. "Before we saw the accident, I was all stressing about going to school today and having Shad Shifferdecker telling everybody how I fell on the ice with the pizzas. Now I can't wait to get there to tell everybody about what we did."

Art grunted over his bowl of Fruit Loops. Even at sixteen, he had to have at least two bowls of them every morning or he griped.

"What?" Lily said.

"I'm sure glad I'm not gonna be there. I bet you tell it until everybody's ready to lose their lunch."

"That would be *ad nauseam,*" Dad muttered. He was looking over a folder full of lecture notes as he ate his bacon and fried egg. Lily was pretty sure Mom could put a roof shingle in front of him and he'd eat it, for all he was aware of when he was getting ready to teach a class.

"What's *ad nauseam?*" Joe said. "We got any more Pop Tarts?"

"Pantry," Mom said.

"When something goes on until everyone is nauseated," Dad said.

"Oh, like till they hurl," Joe said, and proceeded to pretend he was throwing up onto his plate.

"No one is going to throw up," Lily said.

"Except maybe that Chad Whiffenpoof kid," Mom said.

"Shad Shifferdecker," Lily said. "And I'm not telling *him* anything."

But as it turned out, Lily couldn't help but tell him. It just worked out that way.

In the first place, she was later than usual getting to school because it was snowing and Dad said he'd drive her and Joe to Cedar Hills Elementary instead of them walking, only he couldn't find his glasses for what seemed like forever, and Mom and Art had already left for the high school, where Mom taught P.E., so Dad was their only ride, and then when they *did* get going, Dad got so busy telling them about the new thing he'd just read about C. S. Lewis, he missed the turn to the school complex and had to go around the block.

"I don't mind bein' late," Joe said, his brown-eyes-like-Mom's twinkling. "I might even miss the spelling test."

I'm going to miss telling about my adventure before school starts, Lily thought anxiously.

In fact, when she walked in the door, class had already started, and Ms. Gooch was making the first assignment.

"I want you to write a narrative this morning," she said.

Marcie McCleary's hand shot up before Ms. Gooch could even finish the sentence, as usual. "What's a 'narrative'?" she blurted out.

"Now isn't that amazing, Marcie," Ms. Gooch said. "I was just about to tell the class that." Then one of her black eyebrows went up, and Marcie's hand went down.

Ms. Gooch went on to explain that a narrative was the telling of something that had happened. "I want you to choose something important that you've experienced, and then I want you to try to describe it so vividly that we all feel as if we were there when we hear it."

Hands shot up all over the room then. Zooey's plump arm was one of the first.

"What's 'vividly' mean?" she said.

"Who cares?" Daniel said without even raising *his* hand. He was one of Shad's friends, so it figured. "What I wanna know is, do we gotta read it in front of the class?"

Daniel and Leo, Shad's other friend, both looked at Shad as if *he* had the answer to that.

"Some of you will," Ms. Gooch said.

"Can I read mine?" Marcie said.

"You haven't even written it yet." That came from Ashley Adamson, who was one of the prettier girls in the class. She was also one of the ruder, as far as Lily was concerned.

But Ashley's manners didn't bother Lily so much this morning, because Lily already had a wonderful idea. *I'll just write my story about the accident, and then I'll read it to the class, and then everybody will hear it.*

It was so perfect she didn't even wait until everyone quit asking questions and Ms. Gooch told them all to hush up and get to work. Lily had hers half done when most people were still at the pencil sharpener.

When she wrote her final sentence and read over her story, Lily couldn't help smiling to herself. *It sounds even better on paper than it does when I tell it,* she thought. *Ms. Gooch has to let me read mine.*

Just to make sure, she tiptoed up to Mrs. Gooch's desk and whispered to her, "Could I please read mine to the class?"

Ms. Gooch's eyebrow went up again. She could say more with that eyebrow than most people could in a whole sentence. Lily was sure right now it was saying, "What a silly question. Of *course* you can!"

"You're already finished?" Ms. Gooch said. "Most people take the whole time figuring out what to write about!"

"May I?"

Ms. Gooch nodded. Still, Lily was afraid she'd forget, until Ms. Gooch actually called her name. Shad Shifferdecker, of course, yawned loudly, and elaborately arranged his jacket on his desk like a pillow.

He's getting a lot of mileage out of that jacket lately, Lily thought. But she walked proudly to the front of the room and cleared her throat and read her title: "'The Night I Saved the Day.'"

Shad snored. Ms. Gooch raised an eyebrow. Lily's mouth started to go dry.

Maybe this wasn't such a good idea, she thought. After all, she'd even told Mom she wasn't going to let Shad know about what had happened. She ran her tongue nervously over her lips and looked out at the class.

Suzy Wheeler was biting her lip and watching Lily. Behind her, Zooey's round face was pink with anticipation. Across the aisle, Kresha was mouthing something, probably in Croatian.

And there was Reni, sitting tall in her desk—or at least as tall as petite Reni Johnson could sit. Her dimpled coffee-with-cream face was all smiles, and she was nodding her head firmly at Lily.

The Girlz were behind her, especially Reni, and that was all Lily needed to see. She took a deep breath and read on, weaving the story of Thomas and the teenager and the paramedics with her words.

"'And as the ambulance screamed off into the night,'" she read in her last sentence, "'I knew I had somehow helped little Thomas survive.'"

Then Lily let out a breath and realized she'd practically been holding it the whole time. The class was quiet, like they were all holding *their* breaths, too.

Suddenly, Shad's hand went up, and he waved it like he was hailing a lifeguard. Lily's heart skipped. Could it be that Shad Shifferdecker was actually going to ask her a real question?

"What is it, Shad?" Ms. Gooch said.

"Can I read mine now?" Shad said.

Ms. Gooch looked pleased. "Sure, Shad. I thought I'd have to twist your arm to get you up here for something serious."

Shad shot out of his desk and hurried to the front of the room. Lily went slowly to her seat.

That is so unfair, she thought. *Nobody even had a chance to say my paper was good or my experience was cool or even ask any questions. Shad does something right for the first time all year and all of a sudden everybody forgets all about me—*

"You paper was *so* good, Lee-Lee," Kresha whispered to her. "Lee-Lee" was "Lily" in Kresha-language.

Lily nodded a thanks, but she was watching Shad. There was something weird about him volunteering, and as he looked at his paper, he had a gleam in his eye.

"'What I Saw Last Night,'" he read.

Lily's heart sank to her toes.

"'I—was—standing—in—the—pizza place—last night. Who—do—I—see—but somebody I knew—'"

Lily held her breath and waited for her name. Shad didn't say it. Maybe she was wrong about what he had written about—

But in his just-like-a-kid-in-a-second-grade-reading-group way, Shad went on to toil through a description of Lily stumbling out the door with a stack of pizza boxes, supposedly dripping cheese down her leg, and staggering "like she'd had one too many" until she fell flat on top of the pizzas, exposing her underwear to the world.

Shad's paper got a chorus of whistles and clapping from Leo and Daniel, who also tried to give it a standing ovation except that Ms. Gooch stopped them with a disapproving eyebrow. Shad was grinning earlobe to earlobe.

Lily was not. She could feel her face going all blotchy, and she had to force herself not to bury it in her arms on her desk. She stared straight ahead and clutched her hands in her lap.

"That wasn't very nice!" Zooey cried out. "He was making fun of somebody!"

"She didn't say it had to be nice," Ashley said, patting the butterfly clips in her blonde hair. "She just said write about something that happened."

"I did!" Shad said. "I just dressed it up a little."

"There's dressing it up, Shad," said Ms. Gooch, "and there's exaggerating beyond belief just to get a laugh—at someone else's expense, I might add."

"But you have to admit, it *was* funny," Ashley said.

Her friend Chelsea let out her loud shriek of a laugh.

"And he didn't mention anybody's name," said Marcie.

Shad looked blankly at his paper. "I didn't? I meant to—it was Lily Snobbins."

"Shad!" Ms. Gooch said.

"I know—I meant Dobbins."

"It's Robbins!" Marcie said.

"Thank you, Marcie. Now you've both embarrassed Lily," Ms. Gooch said.

"I'd be embarrassed, too, if I showed *my* underwear to everybody in Little Caesar's," Marcie said.

"She did not either show her underwear!"

That came from Reni, who was almost standing up in her desk looking wild-eyed at everybody. Although Lily's face was going from blotchy to solid red, she felt a smile forming inside. Good old Reni.

"I don't think we need to get into the fine points," Ms. Gooch said. "Shad—bad form, pal. Write another paper, and while you're at it, write an apology letter to Lily, too. I want both on my desk by lunchtime. Now, who wants to read next?"

Marcie McCleary bolted out of her desk and headed for the front of the room. While everyone else was rolling his or her eyes, Reni turned to Lily and made her face dimple. Lily smiled back.

Still, as Marcie began to drone on about "The Day I Got Mad at My Little Brother," Lily felt something besides just better-because-my-best-friend-stuck-up-for-me. It was as if something were snapping into place inside her head and fitting in snugly like it was going to be there for a while. That something was a thought:

I have to start my medical career now, so people like Shad Shifferdecker will stop making a fool out of me.

The idea she'd had last night seemed even more brilliant now. She could hardly wait until that afternoon—after school—when the Girlz would meet. Once again she imagined their faces as she announced the next exciting adventure they were going to take together.

"So I think we should add it to our list of rules," she said when they were all gathered in the made-over playhouse in Reni's backyard after school, "that every member of the club has to be trained in basic first aid and CPR."

She waited for the faces she'd imagined. Zooey's going red with excitement. Suzy's shining with quiet anticipation. Kresha's crinkling as she chuckled out Croatian words of praise for Lily. Reni's deepening into admiring dimples.

But Zooey's eyes bulged fearfully. Suzy gave a nervous giggle. Kresha studied the green socks she was wearing with pink jeans.

Lily looked at Reni. She was pulling her chin in and stretching her neck up. It was a sure sign she was getting ready to say something indignant.

"What?" Lily said.

"You want us to learn how to give people mouth-to-mouth resusamatation or whatever it is?" Reni said.

"Yes—and I think it's very important—especially if we ever want to get any respect from people like Shad and those guys—"

"And just how do you expect us to learn that stuff?" she said.

"Yeah!" Kresha said, pumping her head up and down.

Suzy bit at her lip, and Zooey looked like she was going to hold her breath until somebody came up with an answer.

But Lily tossed her hair and frowned at them. "Well, how else? I'm going to teach you," she said.

Although, for the life of her, she had no idea how.

Chapter 4

But Lily didn't waste any time trying to come up with an idea. She told herself that the girls were just blown away at the thought of doing something so adult and serious and that as soon as she got her lesson plans together, they'd be all over it. She started that very evening.

"I want to take a CRP class," she said at the dinner table that night.

"CRP?" Art said, mouth full of spaghetti. "What does that stand for?"

"Can't Write Plain," Joe said.

"No, no. Write starts with a *W*, not an *R*." Dad's blue-like-Lily's eyes got intense, and he picked up his glasses from the side of his place mat and chewed thoughtfully on the earpiece. "It could stand for Chaucer's Rollicking Pilgrimage."

"Children Rolf Plenty," Art said, and then pretended to upchuck his spaghetti.

"Must we reduce everything to regurgitation in this house?" Mom said. "I think Lily's talking about CPR."

"You mean, like mouth to mouth?" Joe said. "Gross!"

"Cardiopulmonary resuscitation," Dad said.

"Relax, Joe," Art said. "Nobody's lips touch."

Joe went back to twirling pasta around his fork. Anything that even came close to kissing got him practically writhing on the floor.

Lily narrowed her eyes coldly at all of them. "It can save a person's life," she said. "And that's what I want to do. Save lives."

"That's very noble, Lilliputian," Dad said.

"I don't even know what noble is," Joe said. "But if you ever think I need CPR, just call a doctor, okay? I don't want to take any chances."

"I'm not going to just learn it on my own!" Lily said. "I want to take classes and learn for real."

"Where is all of this coming from, Lil?" Mom said.

"It doesn't take a rocket scientist to figure that out," Art said. He dumped a ladleful of sauce over his noodles and reached for the Parmesan cheese as if he were preparing his last meal. "It's that whole accident thing."

"So what?" Lily said. She could feel her face going blotchy, and she turned to her mother. Wasn't it about time for Mom to squash Art and Joe down before they started flinging the really ugly comments?

But Mom said, "Is that it, Lil? Did the accident spur this sudden desire to chase ambulances?" She put up her hand before Lily could protest. "I'm sorry," she said. "There's nothing wrong with wanting to help people."

"Thank you," Lily said and gave her brothers a triumphant look.

"But," Mom added, "I'd like to see how long this phase lasts before I try to sign you up for a CPR class. You know how you are with things."

"No—how am I?" Lily said. She could hear her voice getting all pointy the way it did when she was trying to defend herself. It usually didn't work on Mom and Dad, but it was hard not to use it.

"Go take a look at your bedroom," Art said. "It's like a shrine to your I'm-going-to-be-a-supermodel phase."

"Yeah," Joe said. "Last time we had a paper recycling project in Scouts, I went in with all these stupid magazines with girls on the covers with all this lipstick smeared on. They all look like they smell something funny. I had to put them in a paper bag so nobody'd see them."

"I was good at modeling!" Lily protested.

"Yes, you were," Mom said. "You also quit. The point is that whenever you get all jazzed about something, you go all out and that's all we hear about for months—and then, poof, it disappears."

Lily stuffed a hunk of French bread in her mouth so she wouldn't have to answer. *I'm not about to tell them I'm just trying to figure out who I am, just like they've all figured out who they are. They would laugh so hard—I'd have to leave home or something!*

It was true—the part about everyone else in the Robbins family having his or her "thing." Dad was into his C. S. Lewis literature and all that. Mom loved coaching girls' sports almost as much as she loved Baskin Robbins' ice cream. Art was a talented musician, and Joe was a baby-jock.

Only Lily hadn't been able to, as the magazines put it, "find herself." And it bummed her out—a lot—that she hadn't been able to discover the thing that made her shine, inside and out. Sure, she'd been great at modeling, but that hadn't been the one.

But medicine is, I know it, she thought now.

"Uh-oh," Mom said, lips twitching. "The wheels are turning."

"What wheels?" Joe said, looking around the kitchen as if he were expecting to spot a Harley parked on the linoleum.

"The ones in Lily's head."

"What are we in for?" Art said. "Cable reruns of *ER* every night?"

"Are there cable reruns every night?" Lily said.

31

"Yeah." Joe didn't miss a beat as he buttered a slab of bread. "Seven o'clock, channel 30."

"Aw, man—shut up!" Art said.

"What are we doing at seven o'clock?" Dad said, looking, bewildered, around the table.

"Nothing, Hon," Mom said. She winked at the kids.

"So, can I, Mom?" Lily said.

"What—watch *ER*?"

Lily tried not to grit her teeth. "No, take a CPR class."

"I don't even know if you're old enough," Mom said. "Let's wait, huh, and see if this is a passing phase or something you're really into."

I'm into it, Lily thought stubbornly. But she didn't argue. When Mom said, "All right—next topic," the way she did just then, it was time to drop it. As soon as dinner was over, Lily excused herself and made a beeline for the TV so she could watch the rerun of *ER* while Joe and Art took their turns cleaning up the kitchen. Good thing there was a pad and pencil on the table at the end of the sofa. Lily used it to write down words she wanted to look up—like "intubate" and "coding." "He's 'coding'!" a nurse would say, and everybody would scramble all around with concerned looks on their faces.

That night, Lily practiced her concerned look in the bathroom mirror when she was brushing her teeth.

I look like I have a headache, she thought. *I'm gonna have to work on it.*

The next day she got to school early and went to the library and checked out as many first-aid books as the librarian would let her.

"You boys and girls know you can only have two books on the same subject at a time," the librarian said as she looked over the top of her red-framed glasses at Lily. "Are you writing a special report?"

"Something like that," Lily said. She decided she might have to wait until she'd saved a couple of lives before she started talking about her new career to people who weren't likely to understand.

At both recesses, she asked the Girlz to go play without her so she could read up for that afternoon's meeting.

"Read up on what?" Reni said to her.

"Don't you remember what we talked about yesterday?" Lily said.

Reni's neck arched up. "I remember what *you* talked about," she said.

Lily felt a pang somewhere inside. Reni's voice sounded funny—kind of cold or something.

But as soon as they had skipped off to find a spot out of the wind and Lily got her nose into the first book, she forgot about everything else. It talked about the difference between minor injuries and life-threatening ones. Lily skipped right to the life-threatening ones and read about amputated fingers and signs of internal bleeding and diabetic comas. The part about putting a splint on a sprained muscle looked really interesting. She'd have to try it on China tonight....

She was only up to skull fractures by the end of the school day, but she figured she had enough to teach the Girlz in the first afternoon.

However, they ran into some snags that first afternoon.

Zooey, Reni, and Kresha all came in with after-school snacks, and they had to wait while Suzy stopped by her house for a big thermos of hot chocolate Mrs. Wheeler had made for them—and invitations to a sleep-over at their house Saturday night.

"Ooh!" Kresha said as Suzy poured out cups with what to Lily was maddening slowness. "Look good!"

"Hot chocolate *is* good!" Zooey said. "Do you want me to run home and get some marshmallows?"

"You don't need marshmallows," Lily said, and then bit at her lip. "I mean, *we* don't need marshmallows. It probably tastes just fine without them—*great* without them."

Suzy gave her nervous giggle.

"You in a hurry or somethin'?" Reni said to Lily.

33

"We just have a lot to learn," Lily said. "We could run across somebody *today* that needs our help, and we wouldn't be ready."

Zooey's cheerful, round face grew somber. "We could? Why?"

"She's exaggerating, Zooey," Reni said. "Forget it."

"Start to talking, Lee-Lee," Kresha said.

"Well," Lily said, "we need to start with what to have in our first-aid kits."

"What first-aid kits?" Suzy said, thermos suspended in her hand. "Were we supposed to bring a first-aid kit today?"

"No," Lily said patiently, "I'm going to teach you guys how to put one together."

"Where's yours?" Reni said.

"Huh?"

"Don't you have one?"

"Not yet," Lily said. She opened her eyes wide at Reni, who just looked back at her.

"Then how are you going to tell us what to put in one if you don't even have one yourself?" Reni said.

Lily frowned. The rest of the Girlz waited.

"Okay, skip that for now," Lily said. "I'll get mine together and bring it in and show you tomorrow."

"We're doing this again tomorrow?" Reni said.

"Well, yeah, duh!" Lily said. Her patience was slipping away. "It takes more than one day to learn how to take care of people's bodies."

"Ve look at bo-dies?" Kresha gasped. Her sharp little eyes peered out from behind her straggly bangs. "Sound pretty gross to me."

Lily took in a huge breath. "We aren't going to look at them, we're going to learn about them."

"Excuse me, Lily," Suzy said, "but how are we going to learn about them if we don't look at them?"

"What I want to know is—," Reni said, "what if I don't *want* to learn about bodies—not mine—not nobody's?"

A surprised silence seized the inside of the clubhouse. Nobody in it was more astonished than Lily. She stared at Reni, while another pang, a little bigger than the one that morning, rippled through her. Reni just stared back, blinking her big brown eyes.

Finally, Lily got herself to say, "But why wouldn't you want to learn about this stuff?"

"Maybe I would," Reni said. She swept her gaze over the other Girlz. "But wouldn't you all like to have a say in what we do in here?"

"What do you mean?" Lily said.

Reni did the chin-pulled-in thing. "I mean, don't you think you're bein' just a little bit bossy about this?"

Reni looked around again. Nobody nodded—but nobody shook her head, either. The pang inside Lily got bigger. She tried to find a way to slap it aside.

"I'm not being bossy," she said. "I just—" She straightened her shoulders and thought about little Thomas—and about intubation and amputated fingers and starched white coats. "I just have a mission," she said, "and I'm going to accomplish it. I have to. I even talked to God about it."

Lily looked around the clubhouse once more. Heads were so still they looked like they were frozen onto necks.

"Nobody's objecting," Lily said. She couldn't bring herself to say, "except you, Reni."

"Mmm-*mmmm*," Reni said. "All right, then—but I am *not* gonna touch any blood or any throw-up or anything like that."

"Fine," Lily said, tossing her hair. "I'll take care of all the messy stuff. I don't mind."

"There's going to be messy stuff?" Zooey said.

Lily plunged into a reading of the least messy part of the book—the chapter about fainting—so Zooey wouldn't bolt. Then they all practiced pushing each other's heads between their knees, even Reni.

And afterwards, Reni and Lily walked to the corner together like always.

"I guess this is okay," Reni said. "This first-aid stuff."

"I'm not really bossy, am I?" Lily said.

Reni shrugged. "I guess that's just the way you are," she said.

Somehow as Lily hurried home in the cold, almost-dark, that answer didn't make her feel much better.

I'm gonna have to get smart about all this stuff so she won't think I'm just being bossy, she told herself. *I've gotta talk Mom and Dad into letting me take a class. God—can you make this happen?*

God answered—the minute she got home.

Chapter 5

Everyone else was arriving home at the same time. Mom dumped the mail on top of the dryer in the laundry room/mud room, and Dad eyed it longingly as he took off his slush-covered boots. He loved anything that could be read.

"Anything for me?" he said.

"Newsletter from your health club," Mom said.

Art froze, knit cap half off his head. "*Dad* has a *health club*?" he said.

"Cool," Joe said. "Do they got basketball courts over there?"

"Yes, they *have* basketball courts," Dad said. He picked up the newsletter and started patting all his pockets for his glasses.

"Since when does *Dad* have a health club?" Art said.

"Since the doctors told him it would help his recovery if he took advantage of some of their facilities," Mom said.

Lily concentrated on folding her scarf and putting it into her coat pocket. She didn't like to think about the night Dad had burned his hands and arms in the kitchen fire.

If I had known then what I'm learning now, she thought, *he might not* have *to recover—*

"Here's a class for you, Lilliputian," Dad said.

Art rolled his doe-eyes. "Oh—now *Lily's* going to the health club. Get the net."

"Art, watch it," Mom said. She looked over Dad's shoulder. "What are you talking about, Hon?"

"Right here. For girls 10 to 13. 'Taking Care of the Body.'"

Lily held her breath. Dad was right—it *was* a class designed *especially* for her. But she was afraid to yell out, "When can I sign up?" and start another big discussion about this being a phase she was going through.

"Sounds good," Mom said. "Saturday mornings at ten o' clock. Can you get up that early, Lil?"

"Are you kidding?" Lily said. "Yes!"

"I'll drop the form off when I go over there tonight," Dad said.

"I still can't believe my father's going to a health club," Art muttered as he went on into the kitchen. "And my sister—this is too weird."

But Lily had no trouble ignoring him. Her head was completely crammed with, *I'm gonna take a class! I'm really gonna know things. I'm gonna save lives!*

The first session was only two days away. At home, Lily practiced putting splints on China's arms and legs with pencils and hair ribbons, just because it would be nice to go into her new class already knowing something. As for the Girlz, Lily suspended first-aid study with them until she could get the "real stuff" from her new teacher.

"They'll probably check out stethoscopes and blood pressure cuffs to us the first day," she told the Girlz. "Then we can have one good club first-aid kit instead of a bunch of junky ones."

Soon talk at the Girlz Only Group meetings turned to the sleepover they were having at Suzy's Saturday night.

"Is there going to be food?" Zooey said.

"How late do we get to stay up?" Reni wanted to know.

Kresha's concern was a little different. Actually, a lot different.

"I vill ask my mama," she said.

"Why didn't you ask her last night?" Reni said.

"Does she want my mother to call her?" Suzy said. She was looking nervous. Whenever things didn't go exactly according to plan, Suzy's eyes got all scared. She reminded Lily of a fragile little porcelain doll at times like that.

"No—it not dat," Kresha said. "Mama, she vork in the night."

"Who stays with you?" Reni said.

"My two brodders."

"You're so lucky," Zooey said. "I bet you get to eat frozen pizza every night."

"Zooey, what does *that* have to do with it?" Reni said.

"Whenever my mom and dad go out and leave us with my brother, we eat frozen pizza. I like Tostino's—you know—their sauce is the best—"

Lily didn't wait for Zooey to be finished—since she had been known to go on about things like pizza for fifteen minutes. "How often does your mother work, Kresha?" Lily said.

"Every night," Kresha said. "No Sunday, but every night other."

She smiled at them and went on chattering about finding a chance to talk to her mother about the sleep-over.

How can she smile? Lily thought. *If I had to be alone with my two brothers every night, I'd be hating it!*

But Kresha did get permission, and by Friday the Girlz had every detail planned out. Zooey was bringing her mother's special brownies. Kresha was going to teach them all some Croatian words. Reni was going to supply the CDs, and Lily promised to bring the blood pressure cuff she was going to get in class so she could take all their blood pressures. They were so excited it was all they could talk about.

39

But although she never would have said it to the Girlz, Lily was even *more* excited about going to her first medical class.

They don't understand how much this means to me, she told herself. *And that's all right. Not everyone knows what their thing is yet.*

She did remember to thank God Friday night in her prayers that she knew what *her* thing was now. *It's so perfect, Lord,* she thought before she dropped off to sleep.

However, "perfect" started to fray a little around the edges when Dad dropped her off at the classroom in the health club the next morning before he went to his whirlpool. It was early, and the door was still locked, so Lily just stood looking at the poster for the class that was taped to the wall in the hallway.

Why are there things like calendars and toothbrushes and shampoo bottles on this poster? she thought. *Where are the stethoscopes and the thermometers?*

She read the course title on the poster: TAKING CARE OF YOUR BODY, FOR GIRLS 10 TO 13.

Taking care of your *body?* she thought. *Dad said it was Taking Care of the Body—somebody else's body—not mine!*

She had already turned on the heel of her boot and was about to go for the whirlpool room when the classroom door opened and a woman with a perm and a pair of earrings shaped like globes poked her head out.

"Hi!" she said. "You must be either Katie, Natalie, or Lillian."

"Lily," Lily said, and then wanted to bite her tongue off. If she hadn't identified herself, she could just run on down the hall and tell Dad this was a *big* mistake. Now she had to let the woman pull her into the classroom, still going on about Katie and Natalie, whoever they were.

"I'm Missy," Globe Earrings said. "Just make yourself comfortable—I'm going to go out and wait for the others—"

Missy went back out into the hall, still on a quest for the mysterious Natalie and Katie. Lily looked around the room and almost groaned out loud.

The overhead projector was turned on, and the words "Symptoms of Puberty" were enlarged on the white classroom wall. On the counter was a stack of handouts with a drawing on them.

Those do look like some part of your body, though, Lily was thinking—just as the door reopened and Missy breezed back in with two girls in tow.

One looked like she was about ten, the other around thirteen. The ten-year-old had one of those embarrassed smiles on her face, like people get when they don't know what else to do. The thirteen-year-old looked as if she'd like to shove the overhead projector through the wall.

She probably could, too, Lily thought as she watched the big girl stomp toward a chair. *I wouldn't want her mad at me.*

As if she had read Lily's mind, the girl turned to her and made a low, growling sound in her throat.

Hair ball? Lily wanted to say—but didn't dare.

"Lillian," Missy said in her too-breezy voice, "this is Katie—" she tapped the embarrassed-looking ten-year-old's head "—and this is Natalie."

When she tried to tap the big girl's head, Natalie jerked away and stared at Missy. Lily expected to see her flip out a switchblade any second.

"All righty, then," Missy said, still sounding way too cheerful. "Let's get started."

"Aren't we going to wait for the rest of the class to get here?" Lily said.

"This *is* the class," Missy said. "Why doesn't everyone have a seat?"

Katie smiled wider.

Natalie growled.

Lily stifled a groan.

Only three people in the class? That meant this class about getting armpit hair and stuff was going to be even *more* embarrassing, because she wouldn't be able to hide behind anybody or let everyone else answer the questions.

That's it, Lily told herself as she selected a chair two seats over from Big Natalie. *I'm not coming back after this. I already know all about* this *stuff anyway. I thought we were going to learn how to set broken legs and stop people from bleeding to death!*

"Come join us, Lillian," Missy said.

She was pointing to the two empty seats between Lily and Natalie.

"Let's get cozy. We'll be like family before this is over."

Katie's smile stiffened. Natalie growled louder. Lily moved over two seats and said, "It's not Lillian—it's Lilliana. Just call me Lily, though."

"Oh, like the flower," Missy said, and then laughed as if she'd just cracked a side splitter.

"Ha ha," Natalie said.

Missy cut off her laugh and dove for the overhead projector.

"All right, since we're all girls here," she said, "I think we can talk openly. How many of you have had any of these symptoms we see here?"

Natalie's growl turned to a snarl. If Missy wasn't careful, Lily thought, she was going to have to put a muzzle on the girl. At least she was smart enough not to call on her.

"Katie, how about you, honey?" she said.

Katie just stared at the list on the wall and shook her head. Lily decided it must be impossible to talk with your mouth frozen into a smile that way.

"I guess that leaves you, Lily," Missy said.

Lily wished Natalie *would* jump out of her chair and bite her so she wouldn't have to answer. But Natalie just sat there glowering, and Missy stood there looking cheerfully expectant.

"I have some of them," Lily managed to say.

"Good! Which ones?"

Which *ones*? Lily looked miserably at the list.

New body hair

Sudden body growth

Long arms and legs

Smaller waist

Rounder hips

The beginnings of breasts

Coarser hair on legs

There wasn't a single one on there she would want to say out loud—especially not *here*.

"Well, you're nice and tall," Missy said. "Have you always been tall, or did you just sprout up like a sunflower recently?"

Lily knew her face wasn't even blotchy. She could feel it just going straight to bright red.

"I don't know," she said. "I guess."

"Well, Natalie, Katie, Lillian, let's see why those changes are taking place in your bodies. Everyone will need one of these."

As Missy passed out the handout sheets Lily had seen on the counter, Lily kept her head down. Maybe if she pretended to be concentrating really hard, Missy wouldn't call on her again. Ever.

"All righty, then," Missy said for about the forty-fifth time, "this is where it all happens, girls. These are your reproductive organs."

Natalie gave a particularly threatening growl that made Lily move to the far edge of her chair, but Missy breezed on.

"Someday, when you want to have babies, you'll be very glad you have all this stuff, but right now it's probably giving you fits. One thing I forgot to put on my list was mood swings. Any of you feel on top of the world one minute and about ready to smack somebody the next? How about you, Natalie?"

"Yeah," Natalie said. "You."

Missy threw back her head and gave a shrill laugh. "Then I guess we'd *better* find out why! You see the spongy-looking areas that have been colored yellow? Those are your ovaries, where all the eggs for your future children are located. They've been there since before you were born—how about *that?*"

Lily tried to look impressed, but her mind was growling louder than Natalie. *If this class isn't over pretty soon, I am* so *going to scream.*

She did manage to keep herself from howling as Missy chirped on cheerfully about the fallopian tubes and the uterus and the hormones that operated them. When she got to the part about those hormones suddenly sprouting out hair in weird places, Lily couldn't sit there any longer. She stood up.

"I *really* have to use the rest room," Lily said, and she escaped out into the hall.

That is it, she told herself firmly. *After today, I am not going back to that class—ever!*

Chapter
6

When the class finally ground to a halt and all three girls bolted out of the room, Lily beat her father to the car. Fortunately there was a program on NPR that he wanted to listen to, so he didn't ask her any questions about the class while they were riding. But when they met Mom and Joe and Art at Taco Bell for lunch, the first thing out of Art's mouth was, "Well—can you do open heart surgery yet?"

"No. Get out of my face," Lily said. "Mom, I want two bean burritos, okay?"

"I want three—and a taco," Joe said,"—and an order of fries."

"French fries, too?" Lily said.

"French fries with Mexican food?" Dad said.

"Dad, this isn't Mexican," Art said. "It's called paying for food poisoning—in fact, ugh—" He strained his face to make it turn purple and grabbed his middle. "I think I have some now—Lily—help me—save me—"

"Knock it off, Art," Mom said. Her mouth wasn't twitching. Her big brown doe-eyes had a rare stern look. "Enough with the picking on Lily. You were being real good about that for a while, and now you're starting up again. What's with it?"

"You really want to know?" Art said. He twisted away from surveying the menu on the wall and looked seriously at Mom.

"This ought to be good," Mom said.

"Go ahead," Dad said. He, too, was looking serious.

Lily leaned in. Art was about to get his for smarting off at the mouth, and she didn't want to miss any of it.

"It's kinda hard not to make fun of her and pick at her and stuff, because she's so bossy all the time. The way she acts like she knows it all makes me want to just get to her once in a while, that's all."

"I am *not* bossy!" Lily said. "What did I say that was bossy?"

"What didn't you say? Joe shouldn't eat French fries if he's going to have a taco. I should get out of your face—"

"Well, you should. And he shouldn't."

Art shrugged. "I rest my case."

Mom looked at Dad, who crossed his arms and cocked his head at Art. "Lily may be a little more assertive than you'd like," Dad said, "but that still doesn't mean that you can—"

Lily didn't hear the rest. She was thinking about how this was the second time in just a few days that somebody had referred to her as "bossy."

Why doesn't anybody understand that I'm only trying to help? she thought. *I wish there was somebody that appreciated it.*

There will *be*, she decided. As soon as she got some more knowledge and could start saving some lives.

It sure wasn't going to happen through that stupid Saturday class. She was going to have to learn things on her own until Mom and Dad let her take a *real* first-aid and CPR class.

"So, Lily, you haven't said how your first class was this morning," Mom said when they were settled at a table.

"It was my *last* class," Lily said.

"What do you mean?" Mom said.

"It wasn't about what I thought it was going to be about."

"She thought it was going to be about performing brain surgery," Art muttered into his burrito supreme.

"What *was* it about?" Dad said.

Lily's head jerked up. "Uh—just stuff—stuff I already know."

"Like what?" Dad said.

"Just—I don't know—"

"I don't understand," Dad said, looking puzzled behind his glasses. "If you were there and you already knew the stuff, then why—"

"Oh," Mom said suddenly. She nudged Dad. "Drop it."

"Oh," Art said. "That."

"What?" Joe said. "I don't get it."

"Doesn't matter, son," Dad said. "Eat your taco."

"But I want to know!"

"No!" Lily said. "Now shut *up!*"

"See, I told you she was bossy," Art said.

"It was a stupid class and I'm not going back. That's all anybody needs to know," Lily said.

"I have to agree with Art on this one," Mom said. "You are being a tad bossy—telling us what you are and aren't going to do."

Lily blinked.

"Remember when you wanted to sign up for this class, we told you no quitting. If you start something, you have to see it all the way through. Then you can quit."

Lily let her burrito drop to its paper. "You mean, I have to go back there until the course is over?"

"That's what I mean," Mom said.

Lily argued with her mother and father about it off and on for the rest of the afternoon, until Mom finally said she couldn't go to the sleep-over at Suzy's if she said another word about it.

"You said this wasn't a phase you were going through," Mom said. "Now prove it."

Lily almost came out with a "But—" until she saw the firmness in her mother's eyes. Art always called it her "coach" look. "If you're out-of-bounds, you're out-of-bounds," that look said, "and there's no sense in arguing about it or I'll put you out of the game completely."

Lily clamped her mouth shut and packed her bag for the sleep-over.

She wasn't that excited about it anymore, though. She knew the Girlz were all going to want to know about the class, and, worse, they were expecting her to show up with a blood pressure cuff.

That's weird, she thought as she walked through the nippy almost-night air to Suzy's house. *First I wanted to talk about it and they didn't want to listen. Now I* don't *want to talk about it, and they're gonna be all over it.*

And they were. As soon as they had turned off the lights in Suzy's room and had the flashlight on—which was the only way to have a decent sleep-over—and had started into Zooey's mother's brownies, they peppered Lily with questions.

"Does a real doctor teach the class?"

"Do you get to go on a field trip to the hospital?"

"Yeah, and watch an operation?"

"Where's the blood pressure thingie?"

Lily flopped back ultra-casually on Suzy's bed and gave a loud yawn. "I'm so tired from that class," she said. "Can we talk about it later? Somebody else pick a topic."

"Guess what happened yesterday," Zooey said. She always had another topic ready.

"Finish chewing that brownie first, would you?" Reni said.

While Zooey was chewing and giggling, Reni turned to Lily. "What's wrong?" she said.

"Nothing," Lily said.

"Nuh-uh. Something's weird."

"Okay—you want to hear what happened?" Zooey said.

Lily sat up and gave Zooey her full attention. She could still feel Reni looking at her.

"What happen?" Kresha said.

"Ashley Adamson started her period!"

"No, she did not!" Reni said.

Suzy gave her little nervous giggle. "How do you know, Zooey?" she said.

"I was in the bathroom when she found it," Zooey said, looking very important. "She came out of the stall all crying and saying, 'Chelsea—I started! What do I do?'"

"Ashley was actually crying?" Lily said.

"I would be, too," Reni said. "That whole period thing is gross. I don't ever want to start mine."

"Is it gross, really?" Zooey said. "Is it, Lily?"

Lily felt like she was back in Missy's class again. But she chewed at the inside of her mouth and said, "I don't know. I haven't gotten mine yet either."

"Whew," Suzy said, giggling, of course. "I thought I was the only one."

"Who cares?" Reni said. "I'll wait as long as God lets me before I have to start wearing those evil-lookin' pads and worrying about getting stuff on the seat of my desk—"

"When I start mine," Zooey said, "I don't want anybody else to know."

"Nobody will," Suzy said. And then her face clouded over. "Will they?"

"The dentist will if you go in to have your teeth cleaned while you're on your period," Reni said.

"What?" Lily said.

"I heard that," Reni said.

"I heard that boys can tell by the way your breath smells," Zooey said. "I'm not getting near Shad Shifferdecker, then. He'll blab it all over the school."

"And if you don't go swimming, people will know why," Suzy said.

Zooey's face wrinkled up. "Why can't you go swimming?"

"Because—" Suzy ducked her head. "You're wearing that big pad. People will see it through your bathing suit—"

"I do not understan," Kresha said suddenly.

They all looked at her. Lily realized Kresha hadn't said a thing since they'd started talking about periods. Her usually sharp face looked fragile, like she was about to cry.

"It's okay, Kresha," Reni said. "I don't understand all of it either—and I don't *want* to."

"No—I do not understan vhat you are talking about," Kresha said.

But before anybody could even begin to sort that sentence out, there was a sharp scratching noise from the direction of the window. All five of them jerked on the bed and let out a chorus of shrieks.

Lily was the first one to recover. "Shhhh, you guys!" she said. "It was just the wind blowing a branch."

But Suzy's eyes were still wide on her china-white face. "What branch?" she said. "There are no bushes out there. My daddy trimmed them all down before winter."

"Then what *was* that?" Reni said.

Zooey started winding up to a scream as they all turned toward the window. Everyone joined her as soon as their eyes hit the glass.

Staring in at them from the darkness were two deformed, hideous faces.

Zooey was immediately up on her feet in the middle of the bed, screaming like a chased chicken. Suzy plastered herself up against the headboard and froze there. Lily heard a slam and knew that Reni had just thrown herself into the closet. Kresha was nowhere to be seen. Lily had her figured for being under the bed.

Lily looked back at the window. The two faces were still there, as hideous as ever. But as Lily watched, she realized there was something not quite human about those faces. She grabbed for the flashlight and swung the beam right at the window.

The faces didn't move. They only shone, like they were made of plastic. Because they were made of plastic. Lily dropped the flashlight.

"They're gonna get us!" Zooey was still screaming. "Somebody help—they're gonna get us!"

Lily wasn't so sure she was wrong, and when the bed started to move under them. Lily grabbed onto Zooey and began to scream with her.

But it was only Kresha, wriggling out from under the bed—and grabbing the flashlight—and stomping toward the window.

"Kresha—get back!" Lily screamed.

But Kresha went straight to the window, flashed the light into the glass once more, and then reached down—and opened the window.

Chapter 7

This time, even Suzy started to scream. Lily grabbed both Suzy and Zooey and held them against her as she shrieked at Kresha, "Don't! You'll get us all killed!"

That brought a fresh set of terrified cries from the closet.

But none of that stopped Kresha. Tossing her almost-blonde hair away from her face, she thrust both lanky arms out the window and grabbed and pulled. In came the upper bodies of two creatures—wearing plastic Halloween masks.

Flashes of things she'd seen on TV went through Lily's head, and she came to life.

"Bop them, Kresha!" she cried. "Bop them with the flashlight!"

She even let go of Zooey and Suzy and leaped from the bed to the floor to help. But as she tried to snatch the flashlight out of Kresha's hand, Kresha grabbed her wrist and said, "No—Lee-Lee! These my brodders!"

The screaming stopped. From the bed, Zooey said in a shaky voice, "Brodders? What's a brodder?"

"Your *brothers?*"

Reni emerged from the closet to stare at the two culprits, just the way Lily and the rest of them were doing. Kresha snatched the masks from their faces to reveal two very young, very sheepish-looking faces and went into a long stream of Croatian that had her eyes flashing and their heads hanging.

"Well, are they stayin'?" Reni said.

"No!" Kresha said fiercely.

"Then could you shove them back out and close that window?" Reni said. "It's freezin' in here!"

Lily realized for the first time that she was starting to shiver, and Suzy's lips looked absolutely blue.

Kresha nodded and gave her two brothers a push. With a yelp they were gone, and she slammed the window shut behind them. Just in time for the bedroom door to open. Suzy's mother put her head in, eyes sprung wide.

"It's okay, Mommy," Suzy said in a hurried voice. "It was just Kresha's brothers teasing us."

"I so sorry," Kresha said. She went to Mrs. Wheeler and put her arms around her. Kresha was always hugging people.

Mrs. Wheeler *wasn't* always hugging people, but she seemed reassured and finally left the room.

"No more screaming, though, girls," she said.

Lily figured there wasn't much screaming in the Wheeler house. Suzy barely talked most of the time, much less shrieked her lungs out the way they'd been doing.

As soon as Mrs. Wheeler was safely down the hall, everybody piled back onto the bed. This time, Kresha was the center of attention.

"How *old* are your brothers?" Zooey said. Her face was still bright red from howling.

"Julius, he ten. Blage, he only nine year old."

"What were they doing out running around at this time of night?" Lily said. "My mother would have Joe's head on a platter if he did something like that."

"My mama she vork in the night," Kresha said.

"Oh, yeah, you told us that," Reni said. She gave Zooey a hard look, just in case she decided to launch into another frozen pizza monologue.

"Vhen I there," Kresha said, "I make them stay in the house. Vhen I not—" She sighed. "They not."

"Huh?" Zooey said.

But Lily understood. "Boys can be such brats," she said. "But they still shouldn't be going around scaring people to death. What if one of us had a heart attack?"

"Didn't you learn what to do in your class today?" Reni said.

Lily felt the blotches coming on. "We didn't get to that part," she said.

"They no hurt nobody," Kresha said. "They scare us—that's nothing. They no run with the—um—how you say—the gangs."

"Yeah, I guess it could be worse," Reni said.

"But tell them to stay away from us," Lily said.

Only now was her heart starting to slow down. Saving people's lives she could handle. But being scared half to death by two little hoodlums? That was something else.

Even though the Girlz stayed awake late that night, Lily still went to church the next day. The rule in the Robbins house was if you spent the night out Saturday night, you still had to go to church, and you had to stay awake. Lily was a little worried about nodding off during the sermon, but it turned out to be one of those where the pastor seemed to be talking just to her.

"Most of us, if we'd been put in prison unfairly the way Joseph was by the pharaoh, would go sulk in a corner until our term was up," Pastor said. "But not Joseph! He took advantage of every opportunity he had in there and told the other prisoners what their dreams meant. In today's terms we call that blooming where you are planted."

The memory of Missy calling Lily a big sunflower flickered through Lily's head, but only for a minute. She was intent on what the pastor said next.

"Let's all be more like Joseph. If we're stuck someplace where we don't want to be—maybe a job or a location—and we can't get out of it, we ought to ask God to help us find a way to bloom there if we can't be transplanted. What are the opportunities to learn or to minister in this place where you don't want to be? Did it ever occur to you that God has you there for a reason?"

Like my body class? Lily thought.

She thought about it all afternoon while she was reading up on sprains and snakebites in her first-aid books and practicing doing more splints on China until every part of his anatomy that stuck out at all had pencils tied onto it with hair ribbons.

If I can't be in a real class, she thought, *maybe God's telling me he wants me in this class to help people.*

Then she snorted out loud. *Help them what? Draw a picture of their insides?*

But she set down her first-aid book and picked up the stuff Missy had given them to take home to prepare for next week.

"There are plenty of ways to help yourself get through all this *so much more easily,*" Missy had told them cheerfully—after adding "pimples" and "body odor" to the puberty list. "Next week we're going to talk about a healthy diet."

At the time, Natalie had grumbled and Lily had told herself firmly that she wouldn't be back next week.

But now she opened one of the pamphlets and looked at the food pyramid that was printed in it.

"Wow," she whispered as she pored over it. "We're supposed to eat three servings of fruit—four servings of veggies? There's no way we do that around here!"

That was when the idea struck her that helping should begin, of course, at home. She started her campaign right away.

I think God must be really proud of me now, she thought as she drew a large version of the food pyramid on some white rolled paper Mom always kept for her girls to make game banners on.

She posted it on the refrigerator before supper and announced that starting tomorrow, they all ought to follow it.

Joe immediately wrinkled up his nose. "Three servings of milk? I hate milk!"

"Milk *products,*" Lily said. "Yogurt, cheese—"

"Ice cream?" Joe said.

Lily tapped the smallest category with her fingernail. "That's way sweet. You aren't supposed to have very many sweets."

"So where do Fruit Loops fit in?" Art said.

"They don't," Lily said. "You need to eat something healthier for breakfast. So should Joe—instead of Pop Tarts. Breakfast is the most important meal of the day."

But Art didn't answer. He was busy writing *Fruit Loops* in the bread group, while Joe added *Cheetos* to the milk group.

"Where does Mountain Dew go?" Joe said.

"That's a fruit," Art said.

Lily sighed loudly. She was going to have to try an awful lot harder—but it was going to be worth it. She might not *save* lives, but she could *change* some—

Her imagination went to work. Who knew whose life she might change if she could get them on a better diet and a fitness program? She'd start with the Girlz, of course, but it could be anybody. It could be the next person she talked to, even—

The doorbell rang and Dad called out from his study, "Is that the phone?"

"I'll get it," Lily said and went back into her dreams as she went for the door.

Yep—it could be the very next person I talk to. It could even be whoever's at the door—

She swung it open, and there stood Shad Shifferdecker.

Well, she thought quickly, *maybe not.*

"Oh," Shad said. "Do you live here?"

"No, we just keep her around here to answer the door for us," Art said as he passed through the foyer behind Lily.

"Yes, I live here," Lily said, rolling her eyes.

"Oh," Shad said again.

Lily had never seen the boy speechless before. Usually smart comments ran out of his mouth like saliva. Right now he was just clutching a cardboard box with a handle and staring at her. Finally, she said, "So . . . what do you want, Shad?"

"Oh," he said for the third time. "I'm sellin' these."

He nodded down at the box.

"What are they?" Lily said.

"Solid milk chocolate," Shad said. His voice sounded automatic, not like the one he used at school. He was still talking out of the side of his mouth the way he always did, but it was like he was saying a speech he had learned, only he was forgetting most of it.

"I'm sellin' 'em for my karate group," he went on. "A dollar a bar—the world's finest chocolate—or something like that."

Lily watched him carefully as he talked. He was sure a skinny, scrawny kid. She'd never really noticed that before. He wasn't wearing his usually baggy pants and huge T-shirt, so she could see how thin he really was. He didn't look all that healthy . . .

This is it, Lily, she told herself. *You have to be willing to help any-body. If you found Shad lying by the side of the road, would you just leave him there, or would you save his life?*

Well—I wouldn't know how to save his life—yet. But I can do this—

"Chocolate isn't good for you," she said. "It's not in one of the food groups on the pyramid, for one thing, and it has caffeine and a whole bunch of sugar, which you don't need and which can actually hurt you—"

"Look, I don't care what they eat in Egypt," Shad said. His beady little eyes gleamed, and he was already starting to sound more like his school self. "I just gotta sell these candy bars."

"We won't be eating any around here anymore," Lily said. "I just started my family on a new eating program today—"

"Forget it," Shad said. "You're too weird."

And he took his box of candy bars back down the front walk.

But Lily wasn't discouraged. It was Shad Shifferdecker after all. She focused her attention that night on the Girlz, and by the time they met in the clubhouse after school the next day, Lily had a fitness plan drawn up for each of the members. After she had handed them out and the Girlz were reading them, Lily quietly took the brownies Suzy had brought that were left over from the party and slid them under the food pyramid poster she'd drawn up especially for the clubhouse wall.

I think we should take down that Beauty and the Beast *poster and put it there,* Lily thought. But she could do that later. She turned to the Girlz.

"Well," she said, "does everyone understand their fitness plan?"

Suzy gave her giggle and put her hands in her lap. "It's fine," she said.

Kresha looked up from her paper and gave a brilliant smile. "Is okay, Lee-Lee."

"Did you actually understand it?" Reni said to her.

Kresha shook her head, but she was still smiling.

"I'll explain it to you," Lily said.

But just then there was a frail little whimper from Zooey.

"What's wrong?" Reni said.

Zooey pointed to her paper. Her round blue eyes were filling up.

"*What?*" Reni said. She never did have too much patience with Zooey.

"This is all I get to eat?" Zooey said. "I'll starve to death!"

"No, you won't, Zooey," Lily said. "It's a 2,000-calorie-a-day diet. That's enough for anyone."

"You put her on a *diet?*" Reni said.

"Well—yeah," Lily said.

"What did you do that for? Look at that, you hurt her feelings!"

Zooey was crying for real now, nose dripping, eyes already red and swelling. Kresha put an arm around her, and Zooey looked up at Lily.

"Do you think I'm fat, Lily?" she said.

"No!" Lily said. "Overweight" was more the term she would have used, but the pitiful look on Zooey's face, and the angry one on Reni's, were enough to get her searching for another one.

"You're just not as—as healthy as you could be, Zooey," Lily said. "Don't you want to feel energetic and full of life?"

Zooey stopped crying and thought about that. "I thought I already did," she said.

"Just try it for one day and see what happens," Lily said. "Now, if everybody will look at the exercise section of your fitness plan—"

Suzy turned dutifully to hers, and Kresha did what Suzy did. Zooey sniffed and muttered, "I still say I'm going to starve to death." Reni just sniffed.

"You all have different things to do at home," Lily said, "but I thought it would be fun if we all did our jogging together."

Zooey's eyes bulged. "We're going to jog?"

"Don't worry about it, Zooey," Reni said. "None of us is gonna leave you behind."

But she looked doubtfully at Lily. Their eyes clinked together the way they had so many times—only Lily didn't feel a friendly spark from Reni's this time. Her eyes were cold, and they clearly said, "I don't like what you did."

Lily sighed as she followed them all to the door for their jog. She'd been having to sigh a lot lately—but what else could she do when nobody else really understood the big picture? It was kind of lonely being the only one who did.

"Okay," Lily called out to the Girlz when she got outside, "follow me. We're going to go around the block—just one time today."

She turned and took off at a nice trot down the sidewalk.

"You can run up there if you want to," Reni said, "but there's nothin' but ice on that sidewalk. I'm runnin' down here."

She jumped off the curb, splashing Kresha's dirty white tennis shoes with slush.

"Hey!" Kresha cried.

She stomped down and set up another splash of slush that hit Reni in the side of the leg.

"Cut it out, you two!" Lily said. "We're supposed to be jogging, not messing around."

"I didn't see that on my 'fitness plan,'" Reni said. Her neck was arching up, her chin was coming in.

"See what?" Lily said.

"That we aren't allowed to have any fun anymore."

Lily tossed her head as she rounded the corner. *Be that way, Reni,* she thought. *But you're gonna thank me for this someday.*

But that thought was snuffed out the minute she finished the turn. Suddenly there were three figures in front of her—all in ski masks—all with their hands stuck out in front of them like they were about to attack.

"EEEE-YAAA!" one of them screamed.

Then all three of them came straight at Lily.

Chapter 8

For a second, Lily froze. Three guys—wearing masks over their faces—running straight at her. She couldn't even scream what was shouting in her head: *They're going to do something awful to me! If I don't stop them—they're going to do something.*

"No!"

The word burst from her like a cork from a bottle—and it seemed to surprise them as much as it surprised her. Without even stopping to think about it, all three of them turned on the slippery sidewalk and beat a retreat in the other direction, slipping and sliding against each other like a flock of ducklings.

At first, Lily just stood there. *Why are they running away?* she thought. *Just because I yelled no? My brothers don't even do that.*

And then it came into her mind as clearly as a photograph. Brothers. Wearing Halloween masks. Just trying to scare their sister and a bunch of her friends.

Reni caught up to her then, breathing like a little locomotive. "Who was *that?*" she said.

"Kresha's brothers again, and some other kid," Lily said. "Come on—let's get them!"

"Those little brats!" Reni cried—and she took off ahead of Lily at a mad gallop.

Kresha rounded the corner just then and grabbed at Lily's scarf just as she was taking off after Reni.

"May I can stop now, Lee-Lee?" she said. "I am so tire—"

Lily didn't give her a chance to answer. "Come on! It's your brothers again. We're gonna catch them—and this time we're not letting them go!"

She grabbed Kresha by the sleeve and started to run again. They'd taken two steps when there was a thin cry from behind them.

"Lily, wait!" It was Suzy, and when Lily turned around, she was waving frantically.

"Come on!" Lily said. "Kresha's brothers are at it again and we're—"

"No!" Suzy cried. Her voice threatened to break like a china teacup. "Zooey fell down. She's hurt!"

The Ragina brothers ran right out of Lily's mind.

"Go get Reni," she told Kresha, and then she raced back around the corner after Suzy.

Zooey was sprawled out on the ground half on and half off the sidewalk, one leg going one way and one the other. The pages of Lily's first-aid books danced in Lily's head, and her heart pounded out a rhythm: *It's time—it's time to use what I know!*

She was so excited, she forgot to be careful on the ice and slid toward Zooey on one heel. Her entrance into her first real emergency situation wasn't graceful, but she could work on that. Right now, she put on her concerned face and squatted down beside Zooey.

"What happened?" she said briskly to Suzy as she unlaced Zooey's boot.

"That hurts!" Zooey wailed.

"I don't know," Suzy said. She was shaking her head so hard, her swingy black hair was going everywhere. "She was trying to run and then all of a sudden she was on the ground!"

"Uh-huh," Lily said. She gave the boot a final, gentle tug and it came off with a howl from Zooey that was sure to bring every dog in the neighborhood.

"I'm going to hike up your sweatpants leg so I can see what I'm doing," Lily said.

"What *are* you doing?" Reni said. She knelt down next to Lily, huffing and puffing.

"I'm checking her ankle," Lily said. "Just as I thought—it looks like a sprain."

She tried not to sound too excited, but it was, after all, one of the things she'd just been studying about.

"How can you tell?" Reni said.

"See the way her foot is bent inward?" Lily said. "How bad is the pain, Zooey?"

"It hurts!" Zooey wailed.

"That's the other symptom," Lily said. "Intense pain, especially when you try to move it. Can you move it, Zooey?"

"No-oo-oo!"

"What if I touch it here?"

Lily put her finger lightly on Zooey's ankle, setting up a scream from Zooey that made Kresha cover her ears.

"Do you want me to go get your mom, Zooey?" Suzy said. She was beyond nervous giggling by this time. Lily was sure that nervous crying was coming next.

"No—I can handle this," Lily said. "I just need to put a splint on it and then we can get her to Reni's and put ice on it. She'll need an ice pack for 48 hours—"

"I don't want ice!" Zooey cried. "I want hot chocolate. I'm cold! And it hurts!"

"This'll just take a minute, Zooey," Lily said. "I'll need something . . ." Lily looked around, heart still beating out the excited rhythm—*It's time—it's time!* "Kresha—grab me that big stick. Suzy, Reni—let me have your scarves."

Suzy obediently took hers off. Reni said, "What for?"

"I'll show you," Lily said.

Kresha brought her the stick, and Lily measured it carefully against Zooey's leg. It was plenty long enough—it would do nicely. She slid it under Zooey's leg and then wrapped Suzy's scarf around both it and the leg to tie it in place.

"See," she said, "I need yours for down here."

Reni reluctantly took her scarf off. Lily reminded herself to talk to Reni later about how if she were going to be her assistant—and of course she would be because she was her best friend—she was going to have to follow orders first and ask questions later. The nurses on *ER* didn't ask Dr. Benton *why* he needed the scalpel he asked for. She finished tying Reni's scarf around the splint and said, "How does that feel now, Zooey?"

Zooey just went on wailing about it hurting and about her being cold and wanting hot chocolate—with marshmallows.

"Now what?" Reni said.

Lily looked at her quickly. She wasn't sounding all impatient and cold now. She really seemed to want to know what Lily had in mind next. Lily stood up and straightened her shoulders.

"If you guys do exactly as I say, we can get her to your house."

"Why don't we just go get her mom?" Suzy said.

"Because we don't need to," Lily said as she pulled Zooey's sweatpants back down over the splint. "I know just how to do this."

She got Kresha and Reni and Suzy to help Zooey stand up on one foot, and then told Zooey to lean on Kresha and Reni on the hurt side while all three of them helped her hop her way to Reni's.

"I'm going to run ahead and get things ready," Lily said, and she took off down the sidewalk. This time, she remembered to get off into the slush so she wouldn't fall down. It wouldn't be good for the doctor to become the patient.

Well, kind of like the doctor, she told herself. *I don't know everything yet. Good thing it wasn't a nosebleed. I haven't gotten to that section.*

Still, she had to admit that splint was pretty good. It looked just like the one in the first-aid book.

At Reni's she burst into the kitchen, nearly startling Mrs. Johnson right off the stool she was standing on to reach a top shelf. Lily reminded herself to remain calm and went at a more sedate pace toward the refrigerator.

"Zooey has a sprained ankle," Lily said. "We're going to need some ice. Do you have a bag of frozen peas? That works best—"

"Where is she?" Mrs. Johnson said. She was already grabbing for her jacket from the back of a kitchen chair.

But before she could get one arm in a sleeve, the door opened again and Kresha, Suzy, and Reni struggled in with Zooey, all their faces looking as pained and red as Zooey's did.

"Good heavens!" Mrs. Johnson said.

"Put her on the couch, guys," Lily said. "I'll get the ice. Keep it elevated."

"Hot chocolate!" Zooey wailed.

"Get her some hot chocolate," Lily barked in Mrs. Johnson's direction.

"Excuse me?" Mrs. Johnson said.

"Um . . . could you please get her some hot chocolate?" Lily said. "Sorry—I just get so involved."

"Yes, you do," Mrs. Johnson said. "First thing I'm going to do is call that child's mother," and she headed for the phone.

"I'm so cold!" Zooey was saying as Lily hurried to the living room. Her voice had dropped from a wail to a whimper, and there were tears trailing down her cheeks.

"You'll get warm in a minute," Lily said. "Or maybe I should check you for hypo—hypo—for frostbite."

"I'm cold because my sweatpants are all wet from being on the ground!" Zooey said.

"Oh," Lily said. She was glad it wasn't hypo-whatever because she couldn't even pronounce it yet.

"Can we take her pants off her, Lily?" Reni said.

Lily stopped thinking about hypo-something and felt her chest expanding. "Sure," she said, "if you're careful with that splint. Maybe we should cut them off—"

"No! These are my favorite!" Zooey said.

Lily gave in and inched Zooey's soaking wet sweatpants down her legs. When she got them to her ankles, Zooey started to cry all over again. Mrs. Johnson picked that moment to come into the living room.

"I couldn't get her mom," she said.

"That's okay," Lily said. "As soon as we get these wet pants off, she'll be fine."

"I'm not fine!" Zooey wailed.

"We'll get you some hot chocolate," Suzy said.

"No—it hurts!"

"Let me take a look at that," Mrs. Johnson said, and then she cocked an eyebrow at Lily. "If *you* don't mind."

Lily felt a pang inside and moved aside so Mrs. Johnson could get closer to Zooey's ankle. She knew her face was going to go blotchy any minute.

She acts like I was just being a show-off or something, Lily thought. *But I know about this stuff!*

"You're really swelling," Mrs. Johnson said.

"That's what the ice is for," Lily said.

"What's your daddy's number at work, Zooey?" Mrs. Johnson said. "I think if we can't get your mama, we'd better get him. You need to go to the hospital and have that x-rayed."

"I don't want to go to the hospital! No—Lily—don't let them take me to the hospital! You fix it!"

"Lily has done enough fixing for today," Mrs. Johnson said. "What's your daddy's number, Zooey?"

Lily's face did go blotchy then. Mrs. Johnson might as well have poked her in the stomach, she felt so deflated. By the time Mrs. Johnson hurried off to the phone, Lily was blinking back hot tears.

"Vhat this for?" Kresha said. She was holding up the bag of peas.

"Is she supposed to eat those?" Reni said.

"We better wait till her dad comes," Suzy said.

Lily swallowed hard. "She was supposed to put them on her ankle to keep the swelling down." She glanced toward the kitchen where Mrs. Johnson was talking on the phone.

"I think you better get her to the emergency room right quick," she was saying. "She's in some serious pain."

All the girls looked doubtfully at the bag of peas—and at Lily.

"Maybe we better go," Suzy said.

Kresha nodded and planted a kiss on Zooey's forehead.

Lily looked at Reni.

"Maybe you better," Reni said. "My mama's squeezing her lips together. When she does that, she's about to yell at somebody."

Lily sighed—and this time it came straight from her heart.

"Okay," she said. "Bye, Zooey. Keep the splint on until you get to the hospital—if Mrs. Johnson will let you."

But Zooey's face crumpled again. "Don't go, Lily!" she said. "They're gonna do weird stuff to me, and you won't! Don't go!"

"It's all right, Zooey," Mrs. Johnson said from the doorway. "Your daddy's on his way, and everything is going to be all right. Lily can go home."

It was a direct order if Lily had ever heard one, and she left.

Chapter 9

All the way home Lily felt the pang go through her, over and over again.

I did everything the book said, she thought as she ducked her head out of the biting-cold wind. *So how come Mrs. Johnson was treating me like that? She made me feel like I was just playing around with something serious. I wasn't!*

It put her in the kind of mood where she just wanted to go to her room by herself and pull all the books out of her bookcases and reorganize them while she thought about it and thought about it until the pangs went away.

But when she walked in the house and smelled the corn dogs, she remembered—it was Family Night.

They'd started a new thing since Christmas: every Monday night the Robbinses would have corn dogs and milk shakes and Rice Krispie treats and Caesar salad and potato skins as a family and play a board game together. The menu was a combination of each person's favorite food, and they took turns choosing the board game. Last Monday had been Dad's turn, and they'd played some dusty old thing from his childhood called "Authors" that only he was good at. Tonight was Joe's turn to pick, so it was sure to be "Pigmania" or something.

Lily groaned. Maybe if she said she didn't feel well they'd let her off.

But then she also remembered that *she* was the one who had suggested the whole thing when they were all making their New Year's resolutions. If she begged off, Joe and Art would think they could, too, and that would leave Mom playing "Authors" with Dad by herself. Lily wouldn't wish that on anybody.

She dragged herself into the kitchen, where Mom was just pulling the potato skins out of the microwave and Art was pouring milk shakes from the blender.

"Where have you been?" Joe said. "You were supposed to make Rice Krispie treats!"

"I was saving someone's life," Lily said as she marched to the cabinet where they kept the cereal.

"Nuh-uh," Joe said.

"Exaggerating just a little, Lil?" Mom said. "Don't bother looking—I picked up some at the Safeway."

"The package kind?" Art said. "Gross."

"Okay, so I wasn't saving her life exactly."

"Duh," Art said. "So where are they, Mom?"

"While you're looking, see if you can find the croutons for my salad," Dad said from the doorway to the laundry room/mud room. He was holding a large bowl of Caesar salad. There was so much going on in the kitchen, he'd probably had to make his contribution to the dinner out there.

"But she sprained her ankle," Lily said, "and I put a splint on it and we got her back to Reni's house."

"Who?" said all four of the Robbins at the same time.

"Zooey," Lily said.

She looked back at them, and suddenly the pangs went away. They had all stopped what they were doing, and they were all looking at her, and for just a second nobody was making a comment like "Nuh-uh!" or "Duh!"

"Are you serious?" Mom said finally.

"Yeah," Lily said.

"No way," Art said. "How'd you know how to make a splint?"

"I studied it in first-aid books," she said. "And I practiced it on some of my old stuffed animals."

Art seemed to think about it for a second, and then had to content himself with, "So, you're the next new resident on *Chicago Hope*," and went back to pouring milk shakes.

Mom and Dad looked at each other and had one of those conversations where neither one of them said anything. When Dad looked at Lily, his eyes lost their vague am-I-still-reading-C. S. Lewis-or-am-I-talking-to-you? look.

"Well, how about that?" he said. "What did you make the splint out of?"

"A big stick and two of those wool scarves the Girlz were wearing."

"All right, Lil!" Mom said. "Next time Joe gets banged up in a ball game, we'll know who to call."

"No thanks," Joe said.

"Mom, he's doing it," Lily said.

"Joe—back off, babe," Mom said.

He did, but the minute Mom turned her back to get the sour cream out of the refrigerator, Joe picked up a corn dog and pelted it toward Lily's head.

"Hey!" Lily cried. "Joe just threw a whole corn dog at me!"

Joe was saved by the ringing of the phone. Mom waved her hand to get everybody to hush up. They were all quiet as they finished loading up the table with what Dad said was going to be a "gastronomical disaster," but Mom took the phone on its long cord around the corner into the dining room to talk. When she came back, her lips were definitely not twitching.

"Whoa," Art said. "Who died?"

Mom ignored him. "Lil—that was Zooey's mother."

Art nudged Joe. "Here comes the malpractice suit."

"Art," Mom said sternly. "That's enough. Lil—Mrs.Hoffman said they took Zooey to the emergency room and her ankle is broken—in two places."

"Broken?" Lily said.

"Yeah, you know," Joe said, and snapped the offending corn dog in two. Dad glared at him, and he shut up.

"She's more than a little upset," Mom said. "She said she thinks you might have made it worse by having Zooey hobble back to Reni's—which is—well, the point is—"

"The point is, there goes your license to practice medicine," Art said.

"Shut *up!*" Lily cried. The pangs were piling on top of each other, and she couldn't stand to be here with the corn dogs and the smirks and the rude comments another minute. She fled from the kitchen and down the hall to her room. The slamming of her door rattled the house.

Her face was buried in her pillow and she was clinging to China, splints and all, when her mother came in and sat on the edge of her bed. She never did that unless she had bad news—like Lily was being grounded until college or something.

"Your brother has the tact of a Mack truck," Mom said. "He's going to apologize to you."

"I don't care!" Lily cried. "I hurt Zooey!"

"Oh, I don't know," Mom said.

Lily rolled over to look at her. "But her mom said—"

"Zooey's mom says her eating too many Snickers bars when she was pregnant with Zooey is why Zooey is still 'fluffy' to this day—so I don't entirely rely on everything Zooey's mother says. However—"

Lily closed her eyes. *Here it comes,* she thought miserably.

"—in first aid, you always treat for the worst possible injury, just in case. You did the right thing with the splint, but then you should have kept her off of it until someone could come pick her up."

"Oh," Lily said. She turned on her side and stared miserably at China's splints.

"Even better than that," Mom said, "would have been to go and get an adult, instead of trying to handle it yourself."

"But I knew what to do!" Lily said.

"You knew just enough to make you dangerous, Lil," Mom said. She tugged gently at one of Lily's red curls. "I know how you like to go at everything like it's life and death and have it be real. When you were little I could never get you to play store with empty cans and boxes. You had to have the real thing. I'd go to cook dinner and couldn't find a potato or an onion in the place."

"But I'm not a little kid anymore! I *almost* knew what to do, and if I could take a *real* first-aid class, I wouldn't make mistakes like that."

"So now you're a *big* kid and I'm the big kid's mom, and I'm telling her that until that time comes, she doesn't handle any more medical emergencies on her own. Understood?"

"Yeah," Lily said.

"Okay—so come help me beat these guys in 'Pigmania.'"

"Do I have to tonight?" Lily said.

Mom looked at her for a minute, tan face serious, brown doe-eyes searching Lily's face. Finally she said, "Okay—you can skip it tonight. I'll eat your corn dog for you."

When she was gone, Lily rolled back over on her stomach and folded her hands.

"God?" she whispered. "I guess I'm not blooming very well. Would you help me, please? I'm never going to get to be a doctor if I don't get smart about this stuff. Amen."

She opened her eyes, then squeezed them shut again. "And would you please heal Zooey, and don't let her be in pain? I'm sorry—what I did to her—"

The tears wanted to come again, but Lily wiped them firmly away with the backs of her hands and sat up and reached for her first-aid books. If she was going to do this thing, she was going to have to study an awful lot harder.

So she did. Every night that week she hurried to get her homework done so she could go into Mom and Dad's room and watch *Emergency Trauma* on cable on their TV. Those shows weren't made-up stories like *ER*, they were films of the real thing. Sometimes she got so fascinated by what they were doing, she would forget to take notes. Besides, she didn't know how to spell some of the words anyway.

And of course, she kept reading, and she kept monitoring the Girlz's fitness programs to make sure they were staying healthy. All except Zooey. She didn't come to school for several days. When Lily called her house, her mother told Lily, in a voice like a pistol going off, that Zooey could not come to the phone and that Zooey would call *her* when she was able.

"That's funny," Reni said when Lily told her about it. "She let me talk to her."

"Me, too," Suzy said.

"She hang up on me," Kresha said. She flashed her big smile. "She did not understan my English."

"Then why couldn't I talk to her?" Lily said.

Everyone but Reni looked at the floor.

76

"She's probably mad at you for messing up Zooey's ankle more," Reni said.

"But I didn't!" Lily said.

Reni just shrugged. Lily stared at her. She could feel her eyes doing that intense thing that Shad Shifferdecker always said "creeped him out."

"Do *you* think I messed it up more?" Lily said.

"I don't know," Reni said. "My mama says you did—but . . ."

"She does?"

"So does mine," Suzy said in her meek little voice. When Lily looked at her, she hooked her eyes into her lap.

"Mamas," Kresha said. "Sometimes they cray-zee." She circled her finger around her ear, but it didn't make Lily feel any better.

"You saw how I took care of Zooey," Lily said. "I was helping her!"

"Okay, okay," Reni said. "Can we drop it?"

"But this is making me feel really bad," Lily said. "I'm trying to help people and nobody understands that."

She looked around, hoping somebody would tell her she was wrong—that they all understood—that they were behind her one hundred percent. But no one would even look at her. This time, not even Reni.

"I bet if Zooey were here, she'd stick up for me," Lily said. She knew her voice sounded pouty, but there was nothing she could do about it. It just came out that way.

"I guess we'll see," Reni said.

"How?" Lily said.

"She's coming back to school tomorrow."

Reni was right. The next day, Zooey did come to school, armed with crutches and ready to enjoy the attention they got her. She was the first person in the class that year to break a bone, and even Shad

Shifferdecker seemed a little envious. He grabbed her crutches the first chance he got and went racing up and down the aisles with them, until Ms. Gooch came out of her cubicle office and threatened to wrap them around his neck if he didn't put them down.

Lily couldn't wait for the Girlz Only meeting that afternoon—she had to talk to Zooey about her mother at first recess. Ms. Gooch let the Girlz stay in the room with her while everyone else went out.

"I tried to take care of you, Zooey," Lily said when they were all gone. "I hope it wasn't me that made your ankle be so messed up. I don't think it was—"

"I got to have all the ice cream I wanted this week," Zooey said, "and it doesn't hurt that much anymore." She gave her little bow-mouth smile. "My mom cries every time she looks at it, but my dad says she has hormones or something like that."

Lily took a deep breath. "Why wouldn't your mom let you talk to me on the phone?"

Zooey's eyes widened. "You called?" she said. "I didn't know that! Suzy called and Reni called. Oh, and Marcie McCleary called, only I knew she was just being nosy so I didn't tell her anything—but I didn't know you called."

"Then your mom does hate me now," Lily said. Another pang went through her.

"She doesn't hate you," Zooey said. "My mom doesn't hate any-body. She says it's wrong to hate. She wouldn't even let me and my brothers use the word *hate* when we were little kids. She's not so big on that now, since my brothers use worse words and she's busy yelling at them for those."

Kresha's face was twisted into a question mark. "Vhat she talking 'bout?" she said.

"I'm saying my mom doesn't hate Lily. She even said I could go to our Girlz Only meeting—only she said not to jog if Lily tries to make me." Zooey's face shone. "Duh!"

"Oh, I don't know," Reni said. She popped a pencil out of the slot on the desktop and watched it roll down. "It wouldn't surprise me if Dr. Lily-Know-It-All tried that."

The biggest pang yet shot through Lily like a laser. "I would not either do that!" she said.

Suzy's whole face got nervous. "She was just kidding, Lily," she said.

"Yeah," Reni said. "I was just kidding."

But the pang in Lily told her not to be too sure about that.

Chapter 10

The thought that Reni might really have been serious — deep down in the deepest, truest part of her—kept sending pangs through Lily all day long, even during the Girlz Only meeting. Finally that night she couldn't stand it any longer. She had to test it out, so right after supper she called Reni.

"You want to come spend the night Saturday?" Lily said. "Just you and me? We haven't done that since we started the Girlz Only Group."

"Saturday?" Reni said.

"Yeah."

"This Saturday?"

"Yeah."

"This coming Saturday?"

"Yes! Yikes, Reni, yes or no?"

"No."

Lily felt her hand tightening around the phone. "What?" she said.

"I said no. I can't."

"How come?"

"Because—I have something else I have to do."

"What?" Lily said.

"Do you have to know everything?"

It wasn't a pang this time, it was a stab, and it went right through Lily's heart.

"No," Lily said.

"It's just that—"

"Never mind. You don't have to tell me."

"Okay," Reni said.

There was a funny silence on the phone. There was never *any* kind of silence on the phone when the two of them were talking.

"So what are we doing at the meeting tomorrow?" Reni said.

"I was going to teach everybody how to take their pulse," Lily said.

"Oh," Reni said.

"Well, what do *you* want to do?"

"I don't know. Something different for a change."

After they hung up, Lily felt awkward—like she'd just lost her seat in a game of musical chairs. Reni was being cold and sarcastic and weird. Without her warm dimples and her best-friend exchanging of glances, Lily didn't know quite where to put her hands or what to do with her elbows or where to rest her eyes.

I just have to do something, that's all, she thought. *I'll just do— something.*

But no ideas came to her until the next day, and of all people to get one from, it was Ms. Gooch who inspired her.

Ms. Gooch had just returned the class's narrative essays to them, and she told them she wasn't very happy about their work.

"Lily got an A," Zooey said, waving her arms.

"Goody," Shad Shifferdecker said.

Lily turned to glare at him and tried to scoop up a glare from Reni on the way, but Reni just wiggled an eyebrow and turned toward Ms. Gooch. Lily cut the glare short. It was no fun doing it without Reni.

"I think you are all capable of much better than this," Ms. Gooch went on. "I think it's just a case of the January doldrums."

"What's a 'doldrum'?" Marcie McCleary said.

"It's what you get when there's nothing to look forward to, nothing neat to do—Christmas is behind you and it's a long time till summer."

"Oh," Marcie said. "That's depressing."

"Right," said Ms. Gooch, "so I'm going to give you all something to look forward to. We're going to go on a field trip."

The class gave a big gasp as if they were all breathing from the same pair of lungs. But Lily only half listened as Ms. Gooch talked about the Liberty Bell and Independence Hall. She had her idea.

A field trip! That's what the Girlz need! We need to get out of the clubhouse and do something somewhere else—

Ms. Gooch had a hard time settling the class down to their math assignment after her announcement, but Lily hurried right through hers so she could write out the rules to the contest she was thinking up. Whoever could use the nutrition facts on food packages to come up with the most balanced meal in the grocery store would win. She could barely wait for afternoon recess so she could tell the Girlz— well, *some* of what she had in mind.

By then, Zooey had left school to go to a doctor's appointment. Lily and the others gathered in a sunny spot near the bike racks to try to stay warm, although Lily was too jazzed to feel the cold much.

"Who's tired of going to the clubhouse every day and taking pulses and stuff?" Lily said.

Reni's hand shot up Marcie McCleary style. Suzy and Kresha nodded.

"Good," Lily said, "because today we're going to do something different."

"Like what?" Reni said. She wasn't showing her dimples yet as Lily had hoped she would, but Lily kept on.

"We're going on a kind of a field trip," Lily said. "Everybody meet right after school so we can go to the Acme."

"The grocery store?" Suzy said.

"Yeah," Lily said. "And that's all I'm going to tell you. The rest is going to be a surprise."

Reni stomped her feet as she tried to get warm. "What surprise could there be at the grocery store?" she said.

"Ice cream?" Kresha said. "Ve are goin' to have ice cream, Lee-lee?"

Reni stopped stomping. "Oh, yeah, we need ice cream on a day like today."

"No, it isn't ice cream," Lily said. "It's more like—like a treasure hunt. Now that's all I'm going to tell you—"

"Wait a minute," Reni said. Her brown eyes narrowed in the tiny space between her knit cap and her wool scarf. "We're not going to go around reading food packages, are we?"

Lily felt that pang again, only this time she stopped it before it could stab her. "Yes—we are!" she snapped at Reni. "But you don't have to be so—so negative about it!"

Lily waited for Reni to look sorry. She didn't. Lily jammed her fists into the pockets of her jacket and stomped off. She stood by the back door until the end-of-recess bell rang and was the first person into the building.

I don't care. I don't care, she kept telling herself. It was the only way she could keep the pangs from stabbing her.

Still, tears threatened to spill over while she was answering her geography questions, until a figure passed by on her way to the pencil sharpener and dropped a note on Lily's desk, folded up into a triangle the way only she and Reni did it.

All right, it said, *I'll come to the Acme. I didn't mean to make you mad.*

Lily read it three times before she folded it up and carefully tucked it into her jeans pocket. The tears went away.

She'll have a blast once she gets started, Lily told herself. *I know Reni. She will.*

It started to snow just as school was letting out, but it was that light, feathery kind of snow that just fell quietly and didn't stop anybody from doing what they wanted to do, at least not until it was all piled up and the sun went down and it got icy.

It'll be fun walking to the Acme in this, Lily thought as she tucked her jeans legs down into her boots to keep them dry.

Even as she squatted there, three other pairs of boots appeared, and Lily looked up at Kresha, Suzy, and Reni.

"You guys ready?" Lily said.

"Yeah," Reni said, "only I vote we go to Suzy's and slide down her hill in inner tubes. There's gonna be a lot of snow by the time we get there."

Lily stood up slowly. "But I thought you said you'd do the thing at the Acme."

"That was before it started snowing," Reni said. She tilted up her chin in a way Lily had never seen her do before. "I say we go play today and do the Acme tomorrow—or sometime."

Lily looked at Kresha and Suzy. "What about you guys?" she said. "Do you want to go to Suzy's, too?"

"I like to play!" Kresha said, eyes sparkling.

"Suzy?" Lily said.

Suzy glanced nervously at Reni and then back at Lily. She was blinking fast as if she were going to cry.

"Vote how *you* want to vote," Reni said. "Not the way you think somebody wants you to."

"What does *that* mean?" Lily said. Her face was blotching like a red-and-white Dalmatian, she could tell.

"It means she should make up her own mind instead of you making it up for her all the time—"

"I want to go to the Acme," Suzy said quickly. "Please."

Reni pulled in her chin. "Fine. That means we tie."

"No—Zooey's not here," Lily said, "and I know she'd vote with me."

"Of course," Reni said. "That's what I'm talking about."

"So we go to the Acme," Lily said.

"Vhy you are doing this?" Kresha said. Her face was drawn up into a scowl like a WWF wrestler.

Lily stopped. She didn't know why she was getting closer and closer into Reni's face and doubling up her fists and keeping on until she won. Except that Reni was doing it, too. Right now, that seemed like a good enough reason.

"I'm not fightin'," Reni said. Her voice was sounding shrill. "*I don't fight about stupid things like this. Come on—let's go to the stupid Acme. I don't care.*"

She snatched up her backpack and stormed out the door.

"All right, let's go!" Lily said with a smile. But as they all filed out of the classroom, she'd never felt less like smiling in her life.

She'll have a blast once she gets there, Lily assured herself again.

Just to make sure, she fell into step next to Reni as they walked the two blocks to the grocery store and began to explain the contest rules.

"When we get there," Lily said, "you'll have to remember everything I've taught you about a balanced diet. Then I'll give everybody a card—I have them in my backpack—I made them up when I finished geography—anyway, you'll see what you have to find on the card. But it's going to mean reading the backs of the packages to find the proper nutrition—"

"I knew it," Reni muttered.

Lily stopped at the edge of the Acme parking lot and put her hands on her hips. Snow immediately started to land on her eyebrows and lips, but she didn't even brush it off.

"Why are you being so stubborn about this, Reni?" she said. "Don't you *want* to be healthy and fit?"

"I don't know!" Reni said. "Who cares? I'm eleven years old—I got other things to think about. My mama cooks the meals in our house anyway and—"

But Reni didn't have a chance to say what else her mama did. Even as Lily was looking at her, Reni was pelted full in the face with a snowball.

Lily whirled around to see where it had come from, and met with one herself, right up the side of the head. It hit her ear with a smack and ran down her cheek in icy agony.

"What?" Lily cried.

As if in answer, three figures bolted out from behind the big green dumpster and headed straight toward them, bombarding them with snowballs that hit so hard, they took Lily's breath away. She could tell it was doing the same to Kresha and Suzy, because they were both doing some kind of gasping and screaming combination that came out sounding like panicky asthma.

The snowballs continued to come thick and fast and hit harder the closer the attackers came. But even through the onslaught, Lily could see the ski masks that were pulled over their faces, hiding everything but the eyes that sparked with evil.

"It's them again!" she shouted to the Girlz.

But she was cut short by a snowball that hit her square in the lips and half filled her mouth. The ski masks muffled a trio of laughter.

Lily sputtered and spat and got enough snow out of her mouth to shout, "Get 'em this time, Girlz!"

That was one order Reni seemed more than willing to take. She scrambled up from the seat the last snowball had landed her on and without a sound leaped onto the back of one of the three boys.

"Yes!" Lily cried. She lunged toward them.

And then she was on the ground face-down with a wiry figure right on top of her.

"Let go of me, you little creep!" Lily screamed at him.

She managed to get up on her hands and kick her feet at the same time, catching "the little creep" in the seat of his pants with a heel. She hadn't put up with two brothers all these years without learning *something.*

But that didn't stop him from completing his mission. Before she could get the next kick in, he grabbed the back collar of her jacket and yanked on it. Suddenly there was icy misery oozing down her bare back.

"No!" Lily screamed.

She let go with all four limbs and got the kid off of her. By the time she could get herself up, he'd disappeared, and so had one of his cohorts. The only one left was still wrestling with Reni, while Suzy and Kresha clung to each other and giggled hysterically.

"Help her!" Lily said.

"I got him!" Reni said, through clenched teeth.

And for a minute it seemed like she did. The kid had her arms pinned down, but Reni gave a mighty heave and raised them both, surprising his hold loose. But just as she made a grab to pull his ski mask off, he gave her a push with the heels of his hands, and caught her right in the face. Reni fell back, stunned, and the kid took off, yanking and pulling on his ski mask to get it back into place.

"Man—I almost had him!" Reni said.

Suzy and Kresha ran to her to pull her up, but Lily put her arm out to stop them.

"Don't stand up yet, Reni," Lily said. "Not till we see if anything's broken."

"Nothing's broken," Reni said. She hiked herself up and looked frantically around. "Which way did they go?"

"They're gone," Suzy said. "Thank goodness!"

"I want to go after them!" Reni said. "I almost had that one kid's mask off—I almost saw who he was. "

Lily glanced at Kresha. "We *know* who he was," she said. And then as she looked back at Reni, she stopped. "Whoa," she said. "Reni, you're bleeding."

"Where?" Reni said.

"You—um—here!" Kresha said. She put her hands up to her mouth.

Reni put her hand up to her face, but Lily pulled it away. "Don't touch," she said. "It's your mouth. Your lip's bleeding—I hope you didn't lose any teeth. Can I look?"

Reni pulled away.

"Come on," Lily said, "I know what to do this time. My mom talked to me—"

"Don't *touch* me, Lily, okay?" Reni said. She clapped her hand over her bleeding mouth and took a step backward from Lily. "My mom said if I ever got hurt," she said through her fingers, "I wasn't supposed to let you touch me."

Lily was stung so hard, *she* took a step back, too. It was a hurt she couldn't stand. She had to turn it around before it went right through her. With a snap of her head, she turned to Kresha.

"Why is it," Lily said to her, "that every time *your* brothers hurt one of us, *I* end up getting in trouble for it?"

Kresha's frightened eyes suddenly took on a different gleam—a gleam that wasn't scared at all. She drew herself up until she seemed as tall as Lily.

"I know my brodders," she said. "I know how they—" She wiggled around a little, "I know how they—move. Those *not* my brodders."

"But—"

"And those not my brodders other time needer."

Lily folded her arms across her jacket front. "If it were my brothers who were doing it, I'd probably be, like, embarrassed, too, but—"

"Oh, Lily, shut *up!*"

They all turned to stare at Reni. She had her chin pointed straight out at Lily, right along with her eyes.

"Why don't you just shut up?" Reni said again. "You think you know everything—and you don't."

Chapter 11

Then Reni took off at a run toward home, with Kresha trotting right beside her. Lily fought back the tears as she watched them go.

"Lily?" Suzy said beside her. "Are we still going to do the contest?"

Lily shook her head.

"I guess I'll go home then," she said. "You want me to walk with you?"

Again Lily shook her head, and finally Suzy whispered a good-bye and hurried off. To Lily, she looked pretty relieved.

But that wasn't the thing that was splitting Lily's chest in half.

It was Kresha refusing to admit that her brothers were stalking them like little junior terrorists.

No—it wasn't even that. It was Reni—her best friend—saying what she'd said: *Why don't you just shut up? You think you know everything, and you don't.*

All Lily could do all evening was put her hand on her chest and try to breathe. *It feels like something's wrong in there*, she thought.

She even checked her first-aid books for the section on heart attacks, but this didn't feel like what they described. This felt like her heart was breaking. She had never felt worse in her life.

Until the next day. She walked to school without Joe so she could get there early and talk to Reni before the bell rang. Reni wasn't there yet, so Lily sat down in her desk beside Reni's and wrote her a note:

Can we talk? I feel so awful.

Lily told her heart that Reni would write back the way she would have a week ago: *Are you kidding? I feel awful, too.*

Lily folded the note in a Lily/Reni triangle and put it smack in the middle of Reni's desk so she couldn't miss it.

Reni didn't show up before the first warning bell. Lily thought she heard her voice out in the hall once, and once she glanced up and thought she saw Reni's head just disappearing from the doorway. But it couldn't have been, because she would have seen Lily and the note on her desk and she would have come in and they would be all made up by now.

It was only seconds before the final bell when Reni finally slipped into the room. Lily let out a gasp.

Reni's lip was swollen out to twice its size and the skin around it was a painful-looking black and blue. Lily wanted to get out of her seat and run to her and hug her and take a really close look at that lip and ask her if she were putting ice on it and if she'd seen the doctor. One dimple from Reni—one glance that was even a degree warmer—and Lily would have done it.

But Reni wouldn't even meet Lily's eyes as she hurried to her desk, head down.

Still, Lily turned around to give Shad Shifferdecker a warning stare. Making fun of people's injuries was one of his specialties, especially if it happened to a girl.

"What's wrong with you?" Shad said to Lily. "*Dude,* you creep me out when you do that." He turned to Leo. "Doesn't she creep you out when she does that?"

"Just leave her alone," Lily said in her most professional voice.

"Who?" Shad said.

Lily nodded her head toward Reni and once again gave him the warning stare.

"I haven't even done anything!" Shad said.

"Well, just don't," Lily said.

"He probably will now that you've made everybody look at me."

Lily glanced quickly at Reni, who was now facing her.

"Dude—who busted you?" Shad said.

Reni narrowed her eyes at Lily. "Thanks," she said, and she got up and went to Ms. Gooch's desk. The note lay next to Reni's backpack, still in its triangle.

"All right," Lily heard Ms. Gooch say. "But just for today."

Reni came back to her desk, grabbed her backpack, and went up to the front of the room, where she planted herself in the desk Ms. Gooch usually reserved for Shad or Leo or Daniel—or anyone else who was acting up and needed close supervision. Ms. Gooch called it "Being under surveillance."

"What did Reni do wrong?" Marcie said.

"Nothing, Marcie," Ms. Gooch said.

"Then why is she sitting in the survey seat?"

"Surveillance," Ms. Gooch said. "Because she wants to."

Lily caught her breath.

"What did she do to her lip?" Marcie said.

"None of your business," Reni said.

Ms. Gooch cocked an eyebrow. "I couldn't have said it better myself. Now—can we get the day started?"

The day started, and for Lily it seemed as if it would never end. Reni wouldn't talk to Lily or even look at her. She just sat in the most embarrassing seat in the classroom, because she said she wanted to.

She just doesn't want to sit by me, Lily thought miserably.

At recess, when Lily and Suzy were standing in their sunny spot alone, Lily's heart did start to mend a little when she saw Reni and Kresha coming toward them.

But it split apart again when Reni only stopped long enough to say, "We can't have Girlz Only Group at my house anymore. My mama says it's getting too rough."

Lily could hardly get her mouth to move. "Where can we meet, then?"

Reni shrugged. "You decide. You always do."

And then she walked away.

Suzy gave her nervous giggle.

What's so funny? Lily thought. *My best friend hates me now!*

"I have an idea, Lily," Suzy said. "Since it's Friday, why don't we just wait until Monday to have our next meeting? Don't you think Reni will be cooled off by then?"

It was Lily's turn to shrug. "I don't know," she said. "She's never been mad at me before."

But since Suzy was the only one who had a suggestion, and Lily wasn't about to make one and be called a know-it-all again, they did what Suzy said and didn't meet that afternoon. It was the first time since last fall that they'd missed a day after school. Lily didn't know what to do with herself. It only gave her more time to think about everything that was awful.

Reni hating her.

Kresha's brothers stalking them.

Kresha hating her.

And still having to go to that stupid class at the health club—when all she really wanted to do was mope in her room.

It'll just be boring again, she told herself. *And Natalie will be mean and Katie will be silly.*

But I have to—Mom says. It'll be over in an hour and then I can come home and mope.

She even dawdled at the water fountain the next morning so that Missy, Katie, and Natalie were all in the room before she went in, just to cut off some of the time she'd have to spend in there. But when she finally walked in, Lily wasn't so sure she was going to be able to stand it at all.

On the counter there was a box of maxi pads, and the drawings of the ovaries full of eggs and all that other stuff were back. The day had come. Lily froze in the doorway. Why couldn't they learn CPR and the Heimlich maneuver? Blooming where she was planted had done nothing so far, except make her feel like a weed.

"Hi, Lillian," Missy said cheerfully. A pair of miniature Slinkies dangled from her earlobes. "Yeah, would you mind closing that? We're going to get personal in here today."

Wishing she were on the other side of it, Lily closed the door behind her and sank into her seat.

"Not that getting your period is anything to be embarrassed about," Missy was saying. "But at first, like anything else new, it's just a little awkward. What we're going to do today is get you so comfortable with the idea, you won't worry about it for a second longer."

Still smiling like it was Christmas morning, Missy picked up the box of maxipads. Katie began to whimper. Natalie flat out threw her face down into her arms on the desktop.

"Lillian, since you seem to be the most awake today," Missy said, "would you pass this around so you can all have a close look at it?"

Then she put her hand into the box, pulled out a pink pad, and handed it to Lily. Lily stood there looking at it in horror.

"It isn't gonna bite ya," a gravelly voice said. Natalie had perked up and was giving Lily a sideways grin.

"Here," Lily said to Katie.

But Katie shrank back as if it *were* going to sprout teeth and take a leg off. Natalie snatched it out of Lily's hand and inspected it with narrowed eyes.

"I'm supposed to *wear* this thing?" she said. "No way!"

"Sure you are," Missy said. "When that uterine lining starts degenerating, you're going to be glad you have it—"

"I'm gonna degenerate?" Natalie said.

Lily was a little concerned about that herself. She stood next to Natalie and watched as Missy whipped the drawing of the reproductive organs onto the overhead projector and snapped it on.

"Get those lights," Natalie said to Lily. "You can see better when the room's dark."

Yes, ma'am, Lily wanted to say to her. She flipped off the lights and settled uncomfortably into her seat. It was bad enough to have to hear about all this stuff, let alone have to do it next to Lady Wrestler.

"Let me explain again how this works," Missy was saying. "What are these yellow organs here?"

"Ovaries," Lily said.

Natalie grunted.

"Right. And what's stored in these?"

"Eggs," Lily said.

Katie gave an embarrassed whimper.

"Excellent. Now, every month, one of these gets ready to make a baby, and your uterus gets ready to take care of that baby for nine months."

"Not in this body," Natalie said.

"Sure—you'll make a neat mom," Missy said.

Lily looked at Natalie, who looked back at her with the same look Lily knew she had on her own face. Natalie grunted, but it was almost a laugh.

"If a baby isn't made that month," Missy went on, "all that good baby stuff that's now lining your uterus has to be flushed out of your body, so it starts to degenerate and then comes out in the form of what looks like blood. It really isn't all blood, and you only lose about a half a cup during your entire period."

"Gross," Natalie said.

Lily had to agree, but when she turned on the light, Missy was shaking her head at them, Slinkies wiggling.

"It isn't gross, girls," she said. "Sure, it's an inconvenience, but it's part of being a woman."

"It's times like this I wish I was a guy," Natalie said—right to Lily.

"I hear you," Lily said.

She also heard somebody sniffling and looked past Natalie to see that Katie was now crying. Missy fingered a Slinkie and perched on the edge of an empty desk. Her eyes got soft.

"Girls, I'm sorry," she said. "I didn't know you were so scared about getting your periods."

"I'm not scared," Natalie said. "I just don't want to."

"How come?" Missy said.

Natalie scowled at the desktop, then looked at Lily and gave her the lopsided grin. "'Cause I'm scared."

Lily couldn't help laughing. Missy laughed, too, but it didn't come out so-cheerful-it-made-you-gag. It sounded real.

"Partly it's scary because you don't know exactly what it's going to feel like and whether you're going to know what to do, am I right?"

Lily nodded. Natalie looked at her as if she were waiting for a cue, and then she nodded, too. Katie was still crying.

"And partly, I think it's because when you get together with your girlfriends, you all talk about the period horror stories, right?"

"My friends and I don't even talk about it," Natalie said, as if she'd prefer to talk about maggots.

But Lily nodded. "They say everybody'll be able to tell and you won't be able to go swimming and your breath will smell."

"That's a new one on me," Missy said. "We have a lot to talk about." She glanced at her watch. "But some of it can wait until next time. Let me just tell you this: If you think of this as your first step toward being an adult—when you can make your own decisions and be who you want to be and do what you want to do—then it isn't just something to dread. It's cause for celebration."

"You mean, when I get my period I can do whatever I want?" Katie said.

Lily and Natalie exchanged glances that said *Were we ever that naïve?*

"Not quite," Missy said, "but it's a step toward maturity and independence and all those things you're trying to learn. I'll let you in on a little secret." She leaned forward, and all three of the girls leaned toward her. "Being a woman is a beautiful thing. You're going to love it. I think you ought to start planning your celebration now."

"I'm not gonna throw a party," Natalie said. "Then everybody and their brother'll know."

"Throw a private party," Missy said. "Just you and your mom, or you and your sister or some friends. Just another woman or two you want to share this with."

I'm gonna invite the Girlz, of course, Lily thought. And then she was hit with another pang, one that brought the tears back to her eyes.

The Girlz Only Group might be over forever now—now that Reni and Kresha both hate me.

Lily could feel her heart cracking open again. Even when class was over and Natalie punched Lily on the arm and said, "You're pretty cool, you know that?" Lily still hurt.

When it got dark that night, Lily thought about how if Reni were spending the night they would be making popcorn in the microwave and trying to hide from Joe and get Mom to let them keep the light on as late as they wanted. It was too much. If she didn't do something else besides think about Reni, she knew her chest was going to split right open.

She looked at her first-aid books, but they just made it hurt more. All she could see on the pages were Zooey's broken ankle and Reni's swollen lip.

Finally she reached for her notebook, the one she had been taking notes in from *Emergency Trauma,* and began to write. Pretty soon, she had a plan for what she was going to do the first day she started her period.

Missy was right, she decided. When you looked at it her way, it was kind of something to look forward to. She even hunted around in her sock drawer for a quilted thing her grandmother had made her for putting socks and tights in when she traveled—which she had never used—and filled it with the pads her mother had bought for her a couple of months before—"For when it happens, Lil"—and a pair of clean underwear. She tucked the whole thing into the bottom of her backpack.

Now I'm ready if it starts when I'm at school, she thought. *I'm not gonna be caught like Ashley Adamson!*

But even with that done, she still felt empty and lonely and achy. Long before she and Reni would have been ready to give up for the night, Lily dragged China into bed with her and turned out the light.

God, I guess I did something wrong, she prayed. *I hope you forgive me. I hope it's over soon. I won't ever do it again—whatever it was. I miss my friends.*

She fell asleep with a tear trickling into her ear.

When she woke up it was still dark, and it was sleeping-quiet in the house. At first Lily couldn't figure out what had brought her straight up in bed.

Then she heard it. A familiar scratching at the window, like something she'd heard before.

Throwing off the covers, Lily stomped to the window and yanked on her shade to send it spinning to the top. She was ready for the ski masks—

But it wasn't a trio of ski masks that faced her. It wasn't even a pair of silly Halloween faces.

It was two heads—that had no faces at all.

Chapter 12

Lily opened her mouth to scream, but nothing would come out. She couldn't run from the window. She couldn't pick up her first-aid book and hurl it at the glass. She couldn't do any of the things her *mind* screamed at her to do. She just stood there, frozen in horror.

Even as she stared, the faceless faces pressed themselves against the window. There were suddenly features there—distorted eyes and flattened noses and twisted mouths—all smashed by something she could almost see through. Lily's mind stopped screaming and began to talk sense to her.

They aren't Halloween masks and they aren't ski masks. It looks like they have panty hose pulled over their faces.

Lily didn't have to know any more than that. She made a lunge for the window, shouting as she went.

"Get away, you little brats! I know who you are—now get away! You don't scare me!"

Neither of the figures moved. Lily unlocked the window and with a heave yanked it open.

"I said get away!" Lily shouted, right into their faces. At that, the shorter person on the left jumped like a startled squirrel. A second later, he had disappeared.

The other boy tried to shout something, but with his lips flattened inside the panty hose, nothing but smashed-sounding gibberish came out. He leaned back to gape downward, and then he, too scrambled out of sight.

Lily opened the window the rest of the way and leaned out. Both the freezing air and what she saw below made her gasp out loud.

The second boy was just reaching the ground at the bottom of the naked rose trellis. The other one was sprawled out on the ground, arms and legs going in all directions. He wasn't moving.

Even when the other boy squatted down and shook him and shouted something garbled to him through his nylon, the first boy just lay there.

"Is he all right?" Lily shouted down.

The boy's head jerked up. But instead of answering, he sprang to his feet and took off down the walkway. He got his arms tangled up in a holly bush that reached its overgrown branches out of the flowerbed, and he yelped like a puppy. Then he disappeared into the night.

The boy on the ground still wasn't moving, and Lily's heart raced right up her throat.

I have to get down there. I have to see if anything's broken—see if he's breathing—if he has a pulse—

But as Lily tore out her bedroom door and down the hall, the thoughts in her head changed. Just a few hours before, she'd prayed so hard—*I'll never do it again, God, whatever it was—*

And now she was about to.

Her steps changed direction, and she burst into Mom and Dad's room. Mom was already sitting up in bed, rubbing her eyes.

"Lil, what's going on?"

"Somebody was at my window and he fell and he's on the ground outside and he's not moving!"

Lily wasn't sure she was making sense, but it was enough to roust Mom out of bed and get Dad from a dead sleep to a standing position. Her parents were still tying on bathrobes when Lily grabbed three blankets out of the hall closet and took the steps down three at a time. The thoughts pounded in her head as she burst out the back door and ran down the walkway to the fallen boy.

Reni's mom said it was getting too rough—and she was right.

Maybe now Kresha will believe me. They have to do something about these boys now.

Lily skidded to a stop beside the boy. He was wearing a hat and a jacket that was puffed out enough for three sweaters underneath, but Lily could see his legs trembling in the cold. She threw two blankets over him and rolled up the other one in case Mom wanted to use it as a pillow. She didn't do anything else—except pray.

Please, God, don't let him be dead. He's a little brat, but he doesn't deserve to die.

She was trying not to imagine how sad Kresha would be if her brother did have a broken neck or something when Mom got to them and went down on her knees.

"He's unconscious," she said to Dad. "Call 911."

As Dad ran back into the house, Mom ran her hands behind the boy's head, her own head held still and serious.

"I don't think his neck is broken," she said. "Let's see if we can get these nylons off his face. What on earth was he doing up there? He can't be more than ten years old."

"Nine or ten," Lily said. "It's one of Kresha's brothers—"

But as Mom pulled the nylon stocking off of the boy's face, Lily herself yelped like a puppy.

"Oh, Lil," Mom said. "It's Reni."

Chapter
13

For a while, everything was a blur for Lily.

A blur of an ambulance screaming up to the house and drenching the snowy night in flashing red lights. A blur of paramedics with their stretcher and their neck brace, and their official concerned faces. A blur of Mr. and Mrs. Johnson and their terrified ones. A blur of Mom and Dad taking turns holding Lily and telling her it was going to be all right.

But the blur in Lily's own head told her it *wasn't* going to be all right. Her best friend was lying stiller than sleep on a stretcher with a plastic cone over her face and a big plastic cuff around her neck. That wasn't all right. It wasn't all right that the paramedics were saying a smear of things like, "possible skull fracture" and "pulse thready."

But it all suddenly came into focus when they reached the ambulance with Reni on her stretcher and the paramedics were about to slide her in. Lily was running along beside her, craning her neck around the paramedic's blue jacket. That was when she saw Reni's brown eyes flutter open, frightened and darting all around.

"Hey, there," one of the paramedics said. "Glad you could join us."

"You've had an accident—" the other one started to say.

But Reni's voice burst through them, high-pitched and scared. "Lily?" she said.

Lily didn't have a chance to answer. "You can talk to Lily later," the paramedic said. "Let's get you to the hospital first. Your mama's going to ride up front, okay?"

And then they were gone.

"Come on, Lil," Mom said as she put an arm around her. "Let's go have some hot chocolate, huh?"

Lily was too stunned to notice at first that Art was up, in the kitchen, and already had cups of instant hot cocoa coming out of the microwave. By now, only Joe was still sleeping.

"The boy could sleep through a world war," Dad said.

"I think he did," Art said. "What was all that about, anyway? Reni trying to play Spiderman up the side of our house in the middle of the night—"

"What I want to know is what in the world she was doing out by herself at this hour," Mom said. She gave a mug of cocoa a vigorous stirring. "Believe me, Lil, I'd have your hide in a sling if you went that far to get to spend the night with your girlfriend."

Lily looked up dully from the mug Mom set in front of her. "Spend the night?" she said.

"I saw Reni at the 7–11 yesterday. When I told her I was sorry she couldn't spend the night with us, she said her mom wouldn't let her."

"So she sneaks out in the middle of the night by herself so she can do it anyway?" Art said. He poked a couple of numbers on the microwave. "Smart chick."

Once again, the blur cleared and things came into focus. "She wasn't by herself," Lily said.

Dad stopped with his spoon in mid-stir. "What are you saying, Lily?"

"There was somebody else with her," Lily said. "When I woke up there were two faces in the window. I thought it was Kresha's brothers again, so I got up and opened the window, and Reni fell—you don't think she fell because I did that, do you?"

Lily's heart was back in her throat again, splitting her chest on the way up. Dad put his hand on her arm.

"You can just stop your imagination right there, Lilliputian," he said. "Reni fell because of Reni."

"Man, I thought *my* friends were crazy," Art said.

"This isn't crazy. This is just . . . out of control," Mom said. "What's it about, Lil? Do you know?"

Lily pushed her mug away from her. She folded her arms across her chest. But nothing could keep the pangs from turning right at her and stabbing, over and over.

"Talk to us," Dad said.

"It's about Reni hating me now! She says I'm bossy and a know-it-all and I think I'm always right and she hates me so much she got one of Kresha's brothers to come help her try to scare me to death—because she hates me!"

Lily's throat ached with her heart beating there and she wanted to cry so badly, but nothing would come out. She stared into her hot chocolate and wished things would get blurry again, but they were all too clear.

Art finished stirring his cocoa and tapped the spoon on the rim of the mug. "Mostly the kid's right," he said. "You *are* bossy and a know-it-all and you do think you're always right. But that's no reason to hate you. It drives me nuts, but I don't hate you, and I'm your brother. I'm supposed to hate you."

"Thank you, Arthur," Mom said dryly. "I'm sure Lily will thank you for that later."

"Nah—don't mention it."

Dad gave Lily's arm a squeeze. "I don't think Reni hates you. I think she just got a little carried away."

Mom made a soft sound low in her throat. Lily looked up in time to see her parents trade one of those glances.

"You think she's gonna be okay, don't you?" Lily said. "Don't you?"

"She opened her eyes," Mom said. "Good sign."

"She called my name."

"Right. She did."

Lily folded her arms on the table and let her face fall into them. She still couldn't cry. She just felt like she was going to be sick. She'd heard one ambulance siren too many. Seen one more lifeless-looking person than she'd ever wanted to see. Felt this pain in her chest once more than she needed to feel it.

"You need to get to bed, Lil," Mom said. "Come on, I'll go up with you."

"Mom . . . Dad," Lily said as she lifted her head.

They waited.

"I don't think I want to be a doctor anymore."

"Yes!" Art said.

Nobody else said anything. And Lily was asleep almost before Mom helped her into bed.

Lily woke up in the morning just in time to throw on some clothes for church. There had been no word yet about Reni, but the first person Lily spotted when they pulled into the parking lot was Mrs. Johnson.

I don't care whether she hates me or not, Lily thought as she threw the van door into its slide and ran over to meet her. There was frosty air hanging around Mrs. Johnson's mouth and she was stomping her feet the way Reni always did to keep warm. It nearly tore Lily's chest in two again.

"Mrs. Johnson?" Lily said. She stopped a few feet away. "Is she—"

"Where is your mama?" Mrs. Johnson said.

"Please—please just tell me," Lily said. "I know you think I'm a terrible person, but I love Reni. I just want to know—is she okay?"

Mrs. Johnson's eyes popped a little. She dug her hands deep into her coat pockets and moved closer to Lily.

"She's fine, Lily," she said. "She suffered a concussion and some pretty ugly bruises and scratches from your holly bushes, but she's going to come home today."

Lily put her face into her hands and started to cry.

"She's bawlin', Mom," Lily heard Joe say behind her. "You better get over here."

Mom was there in a tapping of boot heels across the parking lot. Mrs. Johnson filled her in while Lily sobbed.

"So I don't get it," Joe said. "If she's gonna be okay, why's Lily cryin'?"

"Don't try to figure it out, man," Art said. "It's just girls."

Mom sent them in with Dad to get some seats. Then she handed Lily a Kleenex, which meant, *stop crying for now and be polite; you can pick it back up later.*

When Lily was finished blowing her nose, she found Mrs. Johnson looking at her as if she were studying her.

"What Reni and her father and I have *not* talked about," Mrs. Johnson said, "is what on earth she was doing *outside* of your house when she was supposed to be *inside* spending the night with you." Mrs. Johnson suddenly looked embarrassed. "From what I heard you tell the paramedics last night, that was not the case."

Lily didn't want to say anything. In fact she couldn't. Reni had lied—had told her mother she was going to spend the night with Lily—so she could come in the night and scare her?

Until then, Lily had clung to the fact that Reni had called out her name when they were putting her into the ambulance. But now—now it looked like her best friend had *planned* her little appearance at the window.

It didn't matter what Art said. Lily knew: Reni hated her. She hated her a lot.

"You don't have to answer that," Mrs. Johnson said. "I think I know. But what I don't understand is how this all got so out of hand. First Zooey is helping you chase someone who supposedly attacked you girls, and she breaks her ankle. Then Reni gets hit in a snowball fight and busts her lip open. Now this." Mrs. Johnson shook her head at Mom. "I just don't know if this girls club thing is a good idea."

It was impossible for Lily to concentrate on the sermon that morning. She sat staring at the pulpit, trying not to let the pangs inside her make her cry again.

There was the hurt pang—because no one understood what the Girlz Only Group had been all about.

And there was the guilty feeling that it was her fault that it had all gone wrong.

And the blotchy-faced feeling that she was an idiot for ever believing it was right in the first place.

I had to have it all my way, and this is what I get, Lily thought miserably. She poked her mom and asked her for another Kleenex.

By the time church was over, Lily's brain was numb from so many awful feelings. But there was one thing that was still going clearly around in a circle up there. It was a question: Who was that other masked figure at her window with Reni?

Lily thought about it that afternoon when she was emptying her first-aid kit and piling up the first-aid books to return them to the library at school.

It couldn't have been Kresha or Suzy, she decided. *In the first place, neither one of them could have climbed up the rose trellis without fainting. And neither one of them would have left Reni lying uncon-scious in the snow, no matter how scared they were of getting caught.*

I taught them better than that, Lily thought sadly. *And besides, they're good people. They're the best.*

Lily swallowed down her hurt and went back to the possibilities.

Maybe she teamed up with one of Kresha's little brothers, she thought.

It seemed too ridiculous to believe, but Reni *had* sort of defended them when Kresha claimed they hadn't attacked the Girlz since that night at Suzy's house.

If she's been planning this, Lily thought, *of course she would try to make me think it wasn't them.*

It was suddenly too sad to think about. Lily dropped the last first-aid book on the stack and sat on the bed hugging her knees to her chest to try to keep it from tearing open again.

But her heart was already broken. Not only had she bossed her best friend so much that Reni would do something like this to get back at her. But she'd also discovered she couldn't save lives the way she'd hoped.

She went ahead and let the tears come this time. There was nobody there to see them anyway. No best friend. No Girlz. Nobody.

There goes another dream, Lily thought. *Who* am *I, anyway, God?*

Lily actually felt her face getting blotchy, lying there all by her-self—because she knew she *wasn't* by herself.

I forgot about God again! she thought, tears trickling into her ears. *God, I'm sorry—again. Will you please help me? Will you help Reni not hate me? Will you help the Girlz Club not to be over?*

She sighed then and asked her last question out loud.

"God, will you please help me find out who I am?"

Chapter 14

Monday, Zooey wasn't in school. She had another appointment with her ankle doctor.

Reni wasn't there either, of course.

Suzy sat very small in her desk and didn't look at Lily once. Neither did Kresha.

It was a lonely day in Ms. Gooch's class.

Even Shad Shifferdecker seemed to be having an off day. He was so restless, going to the pencil sharpener, going out to get drinks of water, wanting to go to the rest room twenty times, Ms. Gooch finally said, "Shad, you're restless as a long-tailed cat in a room full of rocking chairs. Sit down."

At first Lily tried to ignore him, but when he passed Lily's desk for the fortieth time and knocked her pencil onto the floor for the thirtieth, she finally watched him for a minute as he meandered his way back to his seat.

There *was* something different about all his messing around today. He was still poking at Ashley with his newly sharpened pencil and whispering stuff to Marcie to make her shoot up her hand and tattle. But as far as Lily could see, he wasn't enjoying it as much as usual.

On his forty-first trip to the pencil sharpener, Shad paused for a split second at her desk and put his hand on it. Something automatically clicked on in Lily.

He better put some hydrogen peroxide on those scratches, she thought, *or he's going to get an infection.*

She shook her head and went firmly back to her math story problems. *I'm not going to think about things like that anymore. I thought I was this big doctor person and I'm not and I need to get over it.*

Her thoughts tumbled to a halt as she realized Shad had dropped a piece of folded-up paper on her desk. She poked at it with her pencil to be sure there wasn't a spider hidden inside it or something. When nothing crawled out, she opened it.

Did Reni get hirt or something? It said. *Anser here.*

Lily put her pencil immediately to the space Shad had provided for her "anser."

What is that to you? she wrote. *I don't think it's any of your business.*

She put it into her pocket to give to him at recess. No sense getting into note-passing trouble for *him.*

Besides, there wasn't going to be anything else to do at recess.

Before morning recess, Ms. Gooch asked the class to join her in the reading area so she could read aloud.

"It's such a cold, snowy day," she said. "It's perfect for just curling up with a good book."

As Lily dragged herself over to the carpeted section and sat down, she felt the loneliness wrap itself around her. Nothing was any fun when you didn't have any friends to sit with you and—

But suddenly Suzy was there beside her.

"Where's Reni?" she whispered. "Is she sick?"

Of course she'd think that, Lily thought. *Who would automatically think Reni fell out a window and got hurt?*

In fact . . . who would think she got "hirt" at all?

Lily sat up straight and looked around for Shad. He was on the fringes of the group, of course, getting ready to tie Leo's shoelaces together when he wasn't looking.

Why had Shad asked if Reni got hurt instead of whether she was sick? Why would he care at all?

But someone else caught Lily's eye just then, and for the moment she forgot about Shad. Kresha was still sitting in her desk, head down on her arms. Lily really wanted to go over to her—not just because she might be able to "save her life," but because she liked Kresha. Kresha used to be her friend.

Ms. Gooch started to read, and Lily was glad for an excuse to focus her eyes and blink back tears. But focusing was out of the question. In the back, Shad gave an exaggerated yawn. Lily looked at him in disgust.

He was covering his cavern of a mouth with his hand—and even from where she sat, Lily could see the scratches.

Scratches.

Holly bush scratches?

Shad and Reni? Did Reni hate her that much? Lily shook her head. No—that couldn't be.

But if it couldn't, then Lily's heart was breaking right in two for nothing.

The minute the bell rang for recess, Lily bolted from the room and went straight for the rest room. She dove into a stall and slammed the door so she could hide the tears that had hardly waited until she got there to start coming.

"Oh—very bad—very, very bad—" someone whispered from the stall next to hers.

Lily choked back her tears and listened. Someone was crying in soft little sobs.

Lily looked down at the feet she could see beneath the partition. She would have recognized Kresha's sparkle-pink tennis shoes anywhere.

Lily wanted to sink through the floor. *She's probably crying because I accused her brothers—and now I know it wasn't them!*

Lily had thought on Saturday that she had felt as bad as she was ever going to feel. She'd been wrong. There were so many pangs stabbing her, she was afraid to try to say anything to Kresha. The only thing that would hurt more was keeping this all inside.

"Kresha?" she whispered. "Is that you?"

There was no answer. Lily gnawed at her hand for a second and then tried again.

"Kresha—I'm sorry. I wish you'd forgive me."

Whether Kresha forgave her or not was impossible to tell. Kresha just burst into weeping so loud, Lily could barely understand a thing she was saying, even in English.

"I'm sorry, Kresha," Lily said tearfully. "Please don't cry so hard. I'll do anything to make it up to you—"

"Bleeding, Lee-lee!" Kresha cried. "Am I die?"

"What?" Lily said.

But Kresha only started to cry again.

Lily let herself out of her own stall and pulled at the door to Kresha's. When it didn't open, she dropped to the floor and crawled under it. She found Kresha sitting on the edge of the toilet, holding her tummy and rocking back and forth.

"What did you say was wrong?" Lily said.

"I bleeding," Kresha managed to get out. "In my pants—vill I die, Lee-Lee?"

Lily thought she was going to melt into a puddle. "It's your period, Kresha!" she said. "Hasn't your mom told you about your period?"

Kresha stared at her. It only took Lily a minute to remember: Kresha's mother had to work too hard; she was never home to tell Kresha anything. Kresha hadn't even known what they were talking about that night at Suzy's sleep-over, back when the Girlz were all together.

I don't care if there's no group anymore, Lily thought suddenly. *I know what to do, and I'm going to do it for Kresha.*

"You're not going to die, Kresha," she said. She could hear her voice getting calm. "This is normal. It's going to happen once every month from now on, and it means someday you're going to be able to have babies."

Kresha blinked at her. "I vill not die?"

"No! Now wait right here, and I'll be right back. I'm gonna make everything all right, okay?"

Kresha looked at her for a second, and then her face broke into a smile. The teary black eyes were shining already.

Lily dashed back to the classroom, where Ms. Gooch was just locking the door to go out to recess.

"I'm helping Kresha in the bathroom," Lily said. "Can I get my backpack?"

Ms. Gooch didn't ask any questions. She didn't even cock any eyebrow. She just said, "They're dropping like flies now. Sure, Lily—do your thing. Thanks for helping Kresha."

Lily was back in the rest room in a flash and produced a pad and some clean underwear for Kresha.

"You're a woman now, Kresha," Lily said as she waited outside the stall. "I wish I was. I don't have mine yet."

"You going to get, too?" Kresha said.

"Yeah, every woman gets it," Lily said.

Kresha emerged from the stall, and to Lily she already looked older.

"Like a club, Lee-Lee," she said.

"Yeah," Lily said. She started to feel sad again, and she didn't want to go there right now. She linked her arm through Kresha's and gave it a squeeze.

"Since you're the first one of us to get your period, I think we should have a little celebration," Lily said. "Why don't you and me and Suzy do something after school?"

Lily held her breath as she waited for Kresha to answer. Kresha didn't make her wait long. She threw her arms around Lily's neck and laughed.

"I love you, Lee-Lee!" she said.

Lily almost cried again. "I love you—and you know what? I'm sorry I said your brothers were the ones who kept attacking us. I know that wasn't true."

"No, no, no," Kresha said. "Ve vill not talk about that no more."

And they didn't. Instead, they found Suzy and all agreed to meet at 4:00.

"Where?" Suzy said.

Lily took another huge breath. "In front of Reni's house," she said. "And then we'll decide."

School was out at 3:00, and as soon as the bell rang, Lily headed down the sidewalk, praying all the way.

All she could think of to say was *please, God; please, God.* She hoped that was enough. It sure didn't work to *tell* God what she wanted.

Mrs. Johnson answered the door, and she didn't smile when she saw that it was Lily.

"Could I please talk to Reni?" Lily said. "I promise if she gets upset I'll leave right away. I know patients aren't supposed to get upset—"

Mrs. Johnson held up her hand like she was very, very tired. "Go ahead," she said. "She's in her room."

Lily had hoped all the way there that Mrs. Johnson would let her see Reni. But now that she had, Lily's mouth went dry. What if Reni wouldn't talk to her? What if she picked up a stuffed animal or a CD and threw it at her?

By the time Lily tapped on Reni's door, she was imagining Reni standing up on her bed pointing a BB gun at the door.

"Come in," said a voice that didn't even sound like Reni's.

Lily let herself in. She didn't look at Reni until she was beside the bed. When she finally did, Reni wasn't looking at her either.

"Hi," Lily said—at the same time that Reni said, "Hey."

"I'm glad you're okay" and "I'm not as bad off as I look" also came at once.

Lily clamped her mouth shut. So did Reni.

Then they looked at each other.

I'm so sorry, Reni, Lily said with her eyes. *I know I was bossy and stupid—but why would you do that to me?*

I want to tell you, Reni's eyes said. *But I'm afraid.*

"I promise I won't be mad," Lily said.

"Okay," Reni said. She rolled her hands up in the bedsheet. "That day when Zooey fell?"

"Yeah?"

"I suspected it was Shad and Leo and Daniel then."

"Nuh-uh."

"Yuh-huh. I heard Shad tell them at recess that he knew where you lived now because he accidentally went to your house selling karate candy."

"Oh," Lily said.

"He said now they could get you good. You went home first that day before group, remember?"

"Yeah. So he must have followed me to your house from there."

"Yeah."

"But why didn't you tell me you heard that?"

Reni answered with her eyes, and Lily knew.

I was being such a know-it-all—nobody could tell me anything.

"The second time they attacked us, with the snowballs," Reni went on, "I tried to get Shad's mask off so you could all see. That's when he accidentally punched me in the lip."

"That little brat!"

"I knew it was him anyway, just looking in his eyes. But I was so mad at you, Lily, for trying to run our lives and for making Kresha feel bad by saying over and over it was her brothers, I just decided right then to have Shad help me teach you a lesson."

Reni looked down at her hands, now completely rolled up in the sheet like a mummy's. "I guess that wasn't my job," she said. "I shouldn't have done it."

Lily nodded sadly. "I know what you mean," she said. "I was all trying to be this doctor, and I stink at helping people. I'm way too pushy."

"Sometimes you do help people, though," Reni said. She was practically staring a hole through the sheet. "My mom said you wouldn't tell on me—whether I was supposed to be at your house like I told her. Thanks for not tellin' on me."

Lily shrugged. "I guess I helped somebody else. Kresha started her period today."

"No, she did not!"

"Yes, she did, and she didn't know what was happening because her mom never told her about it."

"Nuh-uh!"

"Yuh-huh. I had some pads and clean underwear in my backpack, so she's all right now. We're gonna celebrate in a little while. I wish you could come."

"Have it here!" Reni said.

"Your mom won't let us. She hates me, remember?"

"She never did—she was just a little bit mad at you." Reni winced. "Now she's a *lot* mad at me. But I'm gonna ask her." Then to Lily's surprise, Reni's brown eyes filled up. "I missed you," she said in a tear-husky voice.

It took some talking, but Mrs. Johnson finally gave in to the begging and said they could celebrate Kresha's period there.

"I never heard of throwing a party about it," she said half to herself as she went to the kitchen to scope out the squeeze-cheese supply. "Whatever."

Reni was beside herself. Lily was pretty happy, too, as she opened the front door and motioned for Suzy and Kresha to come in. Suzy was giggling nervously, but Kresha was glowing like the moon.

"No squeeze cheese in here," Mrs. Johnson called out from the kitchen. "I have Ritz Crackers, and I have peanut butter, but no squeeze cheese."

"We have some at my house," Lily said. "I'll run home and get it. Kresha, you sit, like here," she pointed to the Johnson's Lazy-Boy chair, "and be queen for a day—"

"You're doing it, Lily," Reni said.

"Oh," Lily said. "Okay. You guys do whatever. I'll be right back."

On her way to her house, Lily thought about Zooey. It didn't seem right to be throwing a party without her there. As soon as she got home, Lily grabbed the phone and dialed Zooey's number.

"Hi," Lily said when Zooey's mother answered. "This is Lily Robbins. I was wondering if Zooey could—"

"No," Mrs. Hoffman said.

"This isn't like a meeting," Lily said. "We're having a party for one of the girls—Kresha. She's a woman now, she started her period today—"

"I don't want Zooey in this group anymore," Mrs. Hoffman said. "And that's just one more reason. That's the most ridiculous thing I ever heard of." There was a short pause. When Lily didn't say anything, Zooey's mother hung up.

Lily sank onto a kitchen chair. Her heart was tearing in half again.

"She didn't like the idea, huh?" said a voice behind her.

Lily jumped. "What are you doing home?" she said.

"I canceled practice today," Mom said. She patted her stomach. "Cramps."

"Oh," Lily said.

"So, I'm sure you want food."

"Squeeze cheese."

"Three cans in the cabinet there. But don't tell Joe I gave it all to you. I'll be in trouble."

Lily went for the cabinet, but her heart wasn't in it now.

"I think a party's a great idea," Mom said. "I wish I'd thought of that. You haven't started your period yet, have you, Lil?"

Lily shook her head. "No," she said. "I'm not a woman yet. I bet I never will be. I bet I'll never grow up, the way I'm going." Her voice was getting shaky again.

"You have such a strong sense of the dramatic," Mom said, "but I think you're wrong."

Lily pulled out the cans of cheese and held them against her chest, inspecting the tops to avoid looking at her mother.

"Look, I'm sorry Zooey's mother hurt your feelings. Sometimes the consequences of your learning mistakes are pretty painful, but they don't last forever. I know I said you go from one thing to another, whole hog, but I have to say, you always grow when you go through these phases of yours. Just look what you've learned this time."

Lily glanced up. Mom's doe-eyes were bright, but her mouth wasn't twitching. She wasn't teasing this time.

"You've learned to get help when you need it. You've learned to admit your mistakes. You've learned what you *can* do with what you know—look at what you're doing with Kresha."

"You're not just saying that stuff?" Lily said.

Her mother gave a soft snort. "You must be thinking of your other mother or something, Lil," she said. "I never just 'say stuff.'"

Still, Lily shook her head. "I must be doing *something* wrong, though. I prayed and prayed for God to make it work out this time—that I really would end up saving people's lives—and I even tried to bloom where I was planted."

"Bloom where you're . . . ? Never mind. I don't even want to ask." Mom opened the refrigerator and pulled out a jar of olives and some little sweet pickles. "Lil, did it ever occur to you to ask God what *he* wants you to do, instead of giving him all these instructions?"

"Huh?"

Mom put the jars on the counter and opened a cabinet. "I know we've got some cashews back here—I was hiding them from Art. What I'm saying is, you might want to try *asking* God instead of *telling* him. "

Lily felt her brow furrowing. "You mean, I even boss God around?"

Mom's mouth did twitch then. "I'm not even going to go there with you, Lil. Just think about it. Now—here—take this stuff. It'll go great on squeeze cheese and Ritz. Somebody's first period requires at least an olive or two."

Lily's mind was spinning as she stuffed the jars into a bag and made her way back to Reni's.

I really do *tell everybody what to do, don't I?* she thought. *Even God!*

And even he *doesn't like it.*

Wow.

She was going to have to talk to him about that later. Right now, there was a party to be had, and for the first time in what seemed like a long while, Lily actually felt like celebrating.

When she got to Reni's, Kresha was sitting like a queen in the Lazy-Boy chair, and Suzy and Reni had the Ritz crackers all spread out on platters, waiting to be adorned with squeeze cheese.

"Yes!" Lily said. "Let's go for it."

"How many should we make?" Suzy said.

"Not too many," Lily said. "They aren't all that nutritious when you think about it. Let's see." She picked up one of the cans and rolled it to the nutritional information. "See, this has a bunch of additives, artificial coloring—"

"Lily."

Lily looked up. Reni didn't say a word. She didn't have to. *Lily, you're doing it again,* was written all over her face.

Lily put the can down. "Oops," she said.

Reni gave her a grin. Lily gave one back.

And the pieces of her heart came back together.

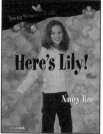

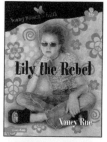

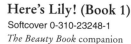

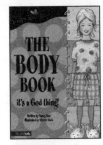

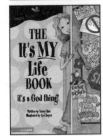

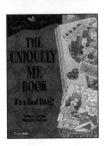

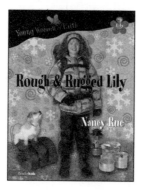
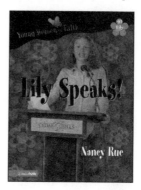